I0545363

Books by T.A. Chase

Dracul's Revenge

Dracul's Blood
Anarchy in Blood

The Four Horsemen

Pestilence
War
Famine
Death
Peace

The Beasor Chronicles

Gypsies
Tramps

Home

No Going Home
Home of His Own
Wishing for a Home
Leaving Home
Home Sweet Home

International Men of Sports

A Sticky Wicket in Bollywood
Chasing the King of the Mountains
At First Touch
Blindsided
Burning Up the Ice

Serving Love at Carnival
A Grand Prix Romance
An Ace in the Tiebreak

Rags to Riches

Remove the Empty Spaces
Close the Distance
Following His Footsteps
Anywhere Tequila Flows
Walking in the Rain
Barefoot Dancing

Delarosa Secrets

Borderline
Snap Decision
Cold Truth

The Blood & Thorn Ranch

Bulls and Blood

Merging Violently

Fall into My Kiss

Every Shattered Dream

Every Shattered Dream: Part One
Every Shattered Dream: Part Two
Every Shattered Dream: Part Three
Every Shattered Dream: Part Four
Every Shattered Dream: Part Five

Sexy Snax

Two for One

Where the Devil Dances

What's His Passion?

Mountains to Climb
Climbing the Savage Mountain

Anthologies

Unconventional at Best
Unconventional in Atlanta
Semper Fidelis
An Unconventional Chicago
Unconventional in San Diego
Aim High

Single Titles

Out of Light into Darkness
The Haunting of St. Xavier
From Slavery to Freedom
The Vanguard
Ninja Cupcakes
Stealing Life
Lassoes and Lust
His Last Client
No Bravery
Always Ready
Possibilities
Ajay's Birthday Gift
The Unicorn Said Yes
Hearts on the Line
Unconventional in Kansas City

Hearts on the Line

ISBN # 978-1-78651-359-5

©Copyright T.A. Chase 2016

Cover Art by Posh Gosh ©Copyright 2016

Interior text design by Claire Siemaszkiewicz

Pride Publishing

Published in 2016 by Pride Publishing, Newland House, The Point, Weaver Road, Lincoln, LN6 3QN, United Kingdom.

HEARTS ON THE LINE

T.A. CHASE

Dedication

I'd like to thank all the soldiers who serve around the world for fighting to keep the rest of us safe.

Chapter One

"Lieutenant Addison," the captain shouted across the room.

Addison glanced up from where he sat with the rest of his unit. They'd arrived at the forward base an hour ago and had been told to wait in the main room for their orders. His men were stripping their gear, making sure everything was in proper working order and ready to go.

"Yes, sir." He walked over to where the captain and the other superior officers gathered.

After saluting, he stood at attention, waiting for the captain to acknowledge him. There had been times when higher-ranking officers had made him waste hours while they talked about trivial shit. Addison fidgeted in his brain, not having the patience for assholes playing mind games. Yet he knew the punishment for not obeying orders, so he had to pay his superiors respect whether he liked them or not.

"Sorry, Addison. Had some last-minute supply lists to go over." Captain Tilton turned to him after only five minutes.

"No problem, sir." Addison wasn't about to complain. Not without knowing Tilton's personality.

The human officers in the army didn't always like dealing with the genetically engineered soldiers. The GE soldiers were stronger, faster and more intelligent than 'true' humans, which bred resentment among the humans.

There was nothing Addison could do about it, except deal with the games the Trues played with him. It annoyed him—he'd never asked to be genetically created for war.

He would reserve judgment on Tilton and the other

humans at the base until he'd been there longer.

"I need you to take your unit into Section Eight." Tilton pointed to the map pinned to the wall.

Addison took one step closer, so he could check the access and exit points. Section Eight looked like it was the closest area to the demilitarized zone. The Unified European Army had started to make incursions into the DMZ, and the American Freedom Front was doing its best to keep them from gaining any more ground.

"Is there anything in particular you're wanting us to look for?" Addison wanted to get all of his orders before he grabbed his men and headed out.

Tilton shook his head. "Nothing specific. I just want to know if there are any UEA around, or any evidence they've been there. We got some intel that the UEA has been making recon missions."

Addison nodded. The UEA was becoming bolder and were moving into AFF territory. They couldn't afford to lose any more, considering their backs were against the wall...or the mountain, as it were.

"All right, sir. We'll gather as much information as we can and bring it back to you."

"I know you will, Addison. The general told me you were the best unit for recon, and I trust his opinion." Tilton nodded when Addison saluted him. "Go to the motor pool and get a couple of Jeeps."

"Yes, sir."

Addison turned sharply and whistled for his unit. All his guys came to their feet, and when he gestured toward the door, they headed in that direction. Baxter led the way, which didn't surprise Addison.

GE soldiers were created in two kinds. Ones like Addison, who were meant to be the leaders of the units, were the intermediates between the Trues and the GEs. For the most part, Addison didn't mind the pressure put on him, but at times he longed for a rest or a chance not to be in charge. The other kind was like Baxter. They were considered the brutes—or merely bodies to throw at the enemies. They did the grunt work of the military.

"Where are we going, sir?" Baxter asked as soon as he joined the rest of the unit.

"To the motor pool to pick up some transportation. Then we're heading to Section Eight for some recon." He glanced at Baxter. "Do you know where the motor pool is?"

Baxter nodded once, then motioned toward the west. "It's on the west end of the base. I studied the map of the base while we flew in here. Also, I know the best way to get to our destination without bothering too many people. To be honest, sir, I don't think we should take vehicles. We should walk in."

The rest of the men didn't say anything because ultimately it wasn't their opinion that mattered. It was Baxter's, and Addison trusted Baxter with his life, so they'd do as Baxter suggested.

"All right, gentlemen, we're going to stop by the armory and make sure we have all the firepower we need, then we'll be walking into the city, making our way to Section Eight. Once we get there, our orders are to look for any sign of the UEA or its agents. We have to find out if they've made it across the DMZ or not."

"Okay."

The rest of the men headed off to the armory, and Baxter fell in step with Addison as he followed behind them. He managed to smile at Baxter without anyone seeing him. There were no rules about being friendly with his fellow soldiers, but he'd seen how other officers—True and GE—treated the grunts like Baxter.

Baxter was a GE as well, but he'd been created as basic cannon fodder to be thrown at the UEA during battle. While Baxter knew that was his purpose, he tried hard to become someone more than he'd been expected to be.

"What are your impressions of Tilton?" Baxter's question was low.

"So far he seems okay, though I'm still reserving judgment

on the man. He might be trying to lull me into believing he's a friend when he's really looking to get rid of us. Of course, I haven't gotten to talk to him that much. We'll have to see the longer we're here. There aren't that many GEs on this base." Addison shrugged. "Tilton might not know whether he likes us or not."

Baxter grunted, showing he understood what Addison was saying. Addison had seen how some of the Trues treated Baxter, like he was a robot that didn't know anything and was only there to serve them. Addison hated his best man being made to think he was less simply because he'd been created, not born.

"We'll get through this together, sir."

"Just like we always have."

They joined the rest of their unit at the armory. The quartermaster gave them all the ammunition they needed, plus a little more firepower than they'd brought with them.

As Addison led his men toward the front gate of the base, he called into headquarters, making sure the lines of communication were open.

"Alpha Two, this is Foxtrot Zulu."

"This is Alpha Two. Go ahead, Foxtrot Zulu."

Addison nodded at Baxter. "We're heading out to our destination on foot. We'll call in when we reach there and before we go silent."

"That's affirmative, Foxtrot Zulu. Continue on your mission. Hear from you when you get to your destination."

Addison turned to his unit. "All right, gentlemen, we're heading out now. Franco, you take point. I'll be rearguard. The rest of you know your spots."

"For about three miles we're in solid AFF controlled territory, but don't let your guard down. Remember, even the most secure area might have spies or assassins waiting to take us out," Baxter told the others.

"Yes, sir," the other six men said before moving off.

Franco took the lead, and the rest spread out until Addison was the last one leaving the base. He nodded at the saluting guard standing next to the gate as they walked by.

He'd done as much research as he could on the area. It was the forwardmost AFF base on the western front, and it had taken the biggest hits from the UEA's offensives, which was why Addison and his unit had been transferred to it. The AFF was losing men at an alarming rate, yet another reason why they'd been sent up to Alpha Two. GEs were more expendable than Trues.

The rest of the American civilians didn't raise a fuss when GEs were killed, and that made the AFF governors happy. They needed public support to continue the war. Not that any of them wished to be conquered by the UEA, but there came a time when the loss of life far outweighed the loss of autonomy, and Addison had a feeling that the civilians were getting to that point.

He shook his head. It wasn't any of his business what the higher-ups decided. Addison and his fellow GEs had been engineered to do as they were told, and if that meant marching into certain death, they would do it.

Addison halted for a second, staring at Baxter's back as his friend strolled ahead. Would he really walk into certain death without once questioning why he had to go? Would he let Baxter go into battle, knowing Baxter would die?

Hell, no! Not if it was Baxter's life, or the lives of any of the men in his unit. Addison didn't see why it was so easy for Trues to sacrifice the GEs who fought beside them. GEs were still human, even if their DNA had been manipulated. They could feel, just like Trues, and fall in love like their real human counterparts.

"Addison."

He glanced up to see Baxter looking back at him. The rest of the unit continued on in front of them. He started jogging to catch up with Baxter.

"Sorry. I was thinking about something."

Baxter chuckled. "You're always thinking. That's what I like about you. I never know what you're going to say to me."

Addison smiled. "And I never know what you'll blurt out, Baxter."

"I try to keep my mouth shut. I'm not smart like you and no one wants to hear what I have to think."

Baxter's words were an insult to himself, but Addison wasn't buying it.

"Remember what I said, Baxter," he reminded his colleague.

Baxter ducked slightly. "I'm not to ever say anything bad about myself."

"Right." Addison slapped Baxter on the shoulder. "You aren't stupid or worthless. You have the right to think what you want."

"As long as it doesn't countermand an order given by a superior officer," Baxter quoted.

Addison bumped his elbow into Baxter's side. "Not necessarily, but I don't want to get into it with you at the moment. Maybe when we have some downtime, I'll try to explain what I mean."

"All right."

"Let's catch up with the others. It's not good for us to get separated."

Baxter jogged easily over the uneven pavement. Addison followed close behind, keeping his eyes open for anything suspicious. No one else was on the street, and Addison brought the map of the city up in his mind. The area they were walking through wasn't populated, or if there were people around, they hadn't been seen by other scout teams.

Addison could feel eyes on him, so he needed to keep on his toes. He whistled softly, and Baxter held up a finger, letting Addison know he'd heard him. Baxter imitated Addison, and the man in front of him did the same as Baxter. It continued down the line until Franco in the front acknowledged they were being watched. Now that they knew about the watchers, they all would keep their eyes open for danger.

As GEs, they could continue at the same pace for hours,

but Addison knew they had only another thirty minutes before they reached Section Eight. He ran up to Franco.

"We need to make a left at the green building at the upcoming corner. That'll take us into the area through an alleyway. Should give us cover to get in. Once we get to the end of the alley, stop. We'll regroup, and I'll give more orders then."

"Yes, sir." Franco nodded.

After Addison dropped back to his spot at the end of the column, he swung his rifle into his hands and checked to make sure there was a round chambered. It didn't pay to go into a strange situation unprepared. Up and down the line, his men were doing the same.

Franco stopped at the corner, then pressed his back to the brick before crouching. He peered around the edge to see if anyone might be waiting for them. By crouching, he made it harder for someone to snipe him. Most people would expect Franco to stay standing while he looked around a corner.

"No one's there," Franco said, as he stood.

"All right. Gephardt, you take point now. Just to the end of the alley, then we'll regroup. I'll assign two-man units to do recon," Addison ordered.

He would keep Baxter with him.

Baxter kept his eyes peeled, which was a quaint, old-time phrase meaning to stay alert for danger. He grinned, having always wanted to use that term, and now he could say he had, even if it was only in his head.

Addison split the unit into teams, and Baxter was happy that he'd be going with the lieutenant. While he liked the other guys, there was something about Addison that set Baxter at ease. It had nothing to do with whether he trusted them or not, but he knew Addison always had his back.

"We'll rendezvous back here at..." Addison paused to check his watch. "Twenty-two hundred."

"Yes, sir," the men all said.

13

"All right. Slip out of this alley two at a time. One group to the right, then one to the left until Baxter and I are the last ones out. Keep your eyes open and stay safe. I want to bring all of you back to base tonight." Addison slapped Franco on the shoulder. "You and Snyder first."

Baxter watched as each team slipped out into Section Eight, until only he and Addison were left. "Do you think we'll find anything this mission?"

Addison kept his eyes on Gephardt and Alves, the previous two to leave. "If we do our job, we will, but we have to be careful."

"Yeah. I can feel them watching us. There's at least three people in the building right across from us." Baxter didn't rest his gaze on the building.

The people who used to call the States their home had been trampled on and caught in the middle of the fighting for ten years, ever since the day the United European Army had invaded, landing all along the east coast. They'd counted on their own military to keep them safe, but after years of fighting wars overseas, the military hadn't had the manpower to deal with the overwhelming numbers the UEA had put in the field.

As the UEA had advanced, the civilians and American Freedom Front had backed up, surrendering ground with each skirmish, until they were backed up against the Rocky Mountains. Civilians were beginning to risk the journey to climb the mountains and get to the other side, where there wasn't any war or death.

Baxter shook his head. There might not be any war over there, but the Western States did their level best to keep refugees from getting into their territory. There were too many already for the land to support, so they protected the borders with deadly force.

"Do you think they'll do anything to us?"

Addison snorted before gesturing for Baxter to take the right side of the street as they stepped from the protection of the alley. They headed straight across the street. Addison had spilt the area into smaller sections for each team to cover. Addison and Baxter's section was the closest, so they hustled to get where they needed to be.

As they made their way from cover to cover, Addison answered him. "The civilians in this section aren't interested in getting involved with us or with the UEA either. So they stayed hidden. We just have to mark them as we go through."

"Yes, sir." And Baxter did as Addison said, marking on the map in his head wherever he spied civilians.

Once they got to their area, they began to do a systematic search of each building and every abandoned vehicle. With True soldiers, such a search could take a day or longer, but with GEs, it took only a total of four hours. Addison and Baxter could scan rooms with one glance, cataloging everything they saw.

As they walked by one building, Baxter looked to his right and saw some posters fluttering in the wind. He scurried over to take a closer look. Addison stayed in the street, not stopping him from doing it. Baxter stared at the old signs.

"Come on, Baxter. Get your ass back here," Addison called.

He jerked, then turned to jog back to his superior officer. When he rejoined Addison, they continued down the sidewalk.

"Could you read those signs?" Addison asked.

"Yeah. They were in old English. The compound I was raised in let us pick any old language we wanted to learn, and I picked old English." Baxter grinned. "It's not hard to figure out once you get the basics down. It's a lot like New English, just the pronunciation's different."

Addison snorted. "What did they say?"

Baxter narrowed his eyes while he translated what he'd just read. Unfortunately, he'd suffered a brain injury during the last big battle they'd fought, and now sometimes he had trouble with words.

"Something about love fading, or some such romantic

nonsense." He shook his head, but not too vigorously. Too violent a movement could cause an episode, and they couldn't afford one of those on this mission.

"Of course love fades. It can get as old and brittle as those posters back there. Love can yellow with time until there's no resemblance to what it once was."

Baxter blinked, then stared at Addison for a second before returning his attention to the last building they had to clear before returning to the rendezvous spot. He hadn't known Addison had such a philosophical streak in him. That was pretty deep thinking for anyone.

They were soldiers, created to be more durable and easily replaceable than Trues. They'd been born in labs and raised at compounds, where they'd trained in every combat style known to man. The compounds were spread across AFF-held country, and each had their own way of educating their soldiers. Maybe Addison's school believed in teaching their kids to think.

It was an odd concept because, aside from processing and figuring out military tactics, none of the GE soldiers were encouraged to think outside the slender parameters of their narrow world of war.

"Can you bring love back when it gets like that?" Baxter wondered aloud.

Addison shrugged, constantly scanning the building they walked through.

"I'm sure sometimes you can. It just takes careful tending and brightening until it's back to its original color." Addison paused.

Baxter wasn't sure if Addison was searching the area around them for people or if he was trying to sort out the thoughts in his head. More than likely, it was both.

They'd been friends and battle partners since they'd been placed in their current unit, and Baxter had learned to listen when Addison talked. A lot of the other soldiers, Trues and GEs, thought Addison was slightly defective because of the way he chose to think before he spoke.

16

Yet Baxter never thought that of Addison. His partner was just as smart as the rest of the soldiers...probably smarter than many. He simply chose not to talk unless he had something important to say.

In fact, Baxter was the defective one after his injury, and he was lucky not to have been removed from the front line units because of it. Usually, when a GE suffered a wound like his, they were taken out of the battle teams and given menial jobs at the different bases.

Addison did talk to Baxter when they were out on patrol on their own. Baxter'd grown used to being puzzled by the things his partner talked about. Baxter freely admitted he wasn't a deep thinker, which was what made him a good GE soldier, but he'd never rise in rank.

Addison would, and Baxter had accepted the fact that at some point, he'd lose his friend to another, bigger unit. He shook his head, not liking to think about that. He tended not to think about the future. Actually, Baxter figured he didn't have many more years in the military. His luck was going to run out at some point. He'd been lucky so far, even though he'd suffered a serious injury a year ago, but he believed there was a bullet out there with his name on it, and he was probably going to find it sooner rather than later.

"But sometimes the paper's too faded and has rips or tears that can never be repaired," Addison continued, after Baxter was sure the conversation was done.

Baxter connected everything Addison said in his mind and nodded. "You're really smart, Addison. Why don't you say shit like that around the other officers? They wouldn't hassle you nearly as much."

Addison shot him a quick glance. "None of those Neanderthals would understand what I was talking about, Baxter. I know you will."

Baxter frowned as he tried to remember what 'Neanderthal' meant. Addison used that word a lot to describe the Trues.

"That's the name of the first humanoid creatures on Earth,

17

right? They weren't very smart." He grinned, proud of the fact he'd figured it out without Addison having to tell him again.

"They were one of the first, but you're right." Addison bumped their shoulders together as they cleared the building then headed outside.

Baxter wished they weren't wearing their body armor. He wanted to feel Addison's skin on his. Baxter turned to look in the opposite direction, keeping watch to make sure they weren't being followed, thankful his helmet covered his head and face.

Those types of longings were anathema among the soldiers. Those kinds of emotions weren't supposed to exist in the GE soldiers. Emotional attachments should have been removed from their DNA.

"Addison," Baxter said.

"Yes, Baxter?"

"Why did you talk the general into keeping me in the unit after my injury? I know it was you. All the others would've packed me for him." It was a question Baxter had wanted to ask since he'd realized what Addison had done for him.

Addison sighed. "Can we talk about this when we get back to base?"

Baxter saw him gesture to the camera in his helmet, and Baxter grimaced at the reminder. All their missions were recorded, in case something was missed in the original search. Also, Addison pointing it out let Baxter know Addison considered their conversation important. He didn't want to risk the chance of someone listening in on it.

"All right."

Addison tapped Baxter's shoulder again, and Baxter ignored how much he wanted to feel Addison's touch. Even if he acknowledged how he felt about Addison, it wouldn't matter. Addison was going places, and Baxter would only hold him back.

"Triple time it, Baxter. We have to get back to the regroup point, then back to base. I think we've got all the information

18

we need at the moment." Addison picked up the pace, and Baxter moved with him.

Baxter had marked all the places where they'd found foreign listening equipment on his mental map. They couldn't say for sure whether it was UEA or some other small rebel faction's eavesdropping devices. All they knew was that it wasn't AFF, and the higher-ups would have to decide what to do with it.

After the entire unit got out of Section Eight, they would stop somewhere and pool all the information each team had gathered. For all his mental faults, Baxter was the best at crunching the numbers and correlating what it all meant. So he would listen to each report, then when they got back to base, he would write his up.

Of course, he'd have Addison go over it to make sure that he'd used the right words and that it made sense.

They were the last team to arrive at the rendezvous point. Addison didn't say anything, simply gestured for Franco to take the lead, and they all moved out. Baxter stayed close to Addison, not wanting to let his friend out of his sight.

This was the first time they'd been at the forward base on which the UEA had been concentrating a great deal of weaponry and manpower. All the spies they had on the other side were saying the UEA was planning something and it had to do with the DMZ.

Baxter was worried that with things changing, they were in more danger than usual, and he wasn't going to let anything happen to Addison if he could help it.

19

Chapter Two

Addison and the rest of the unit returned to Alpha Two base. He sent the rest of the men to find their barracks while he and Baxter reported to the captain. Tilton didn't keep them waiting this time, and though Addison appreciated that, he didn't let down his guard about the captain.

"Report."

Taking a deep breath, Addison started to speak, but Tilton shook his head.

"I know you aren't the recorder for the unit, Lieutenant. Sergeant Baxter, please report what your unit discovered during your mission." Tilton nodded toward Baxter.

Blinking in surprise, Baxter glanced at Addison, who nodded in encouragement. It was rare for Trues to acknowledge Baxter — he was just a grunt in their eyes.

Baxter began to recount everything he'd gathered from all the other men. Addison relaxed slightly, confident Baxter would brief the captain completely.

While Baxter had suffered severe brain trauma during the mission last year, it hadn't seemed to affect his ability to collect and correlate all the information given to him. The one problem he did have was with memories and knowledge he'd had before the injury. It took him a while to recover them, and sometimes he never did.

Thankfully, no one but he and Baxter knew about that issue, especially since Addison had never told anyone, and for some reason, the doctors had never tested for it. More than likely it was because they didn't care about Baxter's mental health. All they wanted was him healthy enough to go out and fight.

"Good job, Sergeant. I'd like you to go to my scribes and have them write down what you told me. That way we'll be able to send a copy to joint chiefs, so they know what you found out there." Tilton gestured toward a group of men, one of whom looked up to wave Baxter over.

Baxter glanced at Addison again, but Addison didn't make any movement. Tilton had issued orders, and Baxter had to obey them, whether either of them liked it or not. Baxter didn't like being away from Addison, and to tell the truth, the lieutenant didn't like having Baxter too far away either.

He shouldn't become so attached to any of the men under his command. Chances were he would outlive them all because he had been engineered to move up the ranks and become a squadron or battalion leader, where he wouldn't have to go out into the field if he didn't want to.

Normally he wouldn't become friends with any of them, and he hadn't done it with the other guys of this unit. Baxter had always been a special case, though, and Addison didn't know what made the sergeant different from the others.

Addison shifted his gaze to the man, then back to Baxter.

"Yes, sir." Baxter saluted Tilton, then moved to where the scribes sat.

"I need to discuss something with you, Lieutenant. Come with me."

He followed the captain from the main room to where his office was. Tilton waited for Addison to walk into the room before he shut the door. He motioned to a chair in front of his desk, and Addison took it.

After sitting at the very edge of the seat, he kept his back ramrod straight and rested his hands on his knees. It was rare for a superior officer to talk one on one with any of the soldiers under him, and even rarer for a True to talk to a GE personally.

Tilton took a seat behind the desk, then propped his elbows on the surface. He studied Addison, and Addison didn't blink or move a muscle. If it was a staring contest or

21

merely a waiting game, Addison would win. He'd learned how to do it from an early age.

He didn't know if Tilton expected him to break or not, but better men than the captain had tried...and failed.

"Addison," Tilton finally spoke.

"Yes, sir," Addison replied, not caring how insolent he sounded. He'd been getting the feeling Tilton needed him and his men more than Addison needed Tilton.

"I've been hearing some rumors about you and your unit. When some of the other commanders heard you'd been transferred here, they inundated me with helpful information."

Addison didn't reply to those statements. He wasn't surprised. All of the GEs had files, and whenever they did anything, it was reported. The scientists were determined to gather as much data as they could from this long-term experiment. They discovered new ways to improve the GEs with each battle and each injury the GEs received.

He disliked being a lab rat, though he knew he wasn't supposed to have feelings about his place in the world. He couldn't say anything because they wouldn't listen to him, and they didn't care what he thought.

"Some of them believe you're one of the best GE commanders out there. Others believe you're a time bomb waiting for the right moment to explode. You're too good at your job, and they're worried you're going to try to take their place."

"Why would I do that?" Addison couldn't help but ask.

"Because they're idiots and terrible officers. They think everyone, whether he's a True or a GE, is out to get them. But I also believe those who think your shit don't stink are the ones who think GEs are the evolutionary next step." Tilton shrugged.

"Which are you?" To be totally honest, Addison wasn't interested in the answer. He simply wanted the conversation over with so that he could go and find Baxter, then gather the rest of his unit for their evening meal.

"I'm refraining from having an opinion at the moment. I'll watch how your unit does while you're here, and when it's time for you to move on, I'll put my thoughts in your file." Tilton grimaced. "I don't like you, but it has nothing to with you being a GE."

Addison mentally rolled his eyes. Of course it had nothing to do with them being GEs and everything to do with Tilton being told what he should think. *Christ! The man must think I'm an idiot as well.*

"If you say so, sir." Addison wasn't really interested in all the other bullshit going on around him. He wanted to live his life as best he could while being continuously shot at and belittled by people who assumed they were better than he was.

"Are you mouthing off to me?" Tilton glared at him.

"No, sir." Addison kept any sort of insubordination out of his voice. It didn't pay to piss off the captain on the first day.

"I'm keeping my eye on you and your unit, Addison. I haven't judged you as a waste of air and food yet. You completed your mission in a timely fashion and brought back important information. But if you push me, I'll split you all up and send you out on missions behind enemy lines," Tilton threatened. "Dismissed."

After saluting, Addison left Tilton's office. He walked out into the main room, searching for Baxter. His friend was leaning against the far wall, arms crossed, watching the people milling around. Addison noticed that they gave Baxter a wide berth, never coming close enough for him either to say something to them or for them to come into contact with him.

Baxter showed no reaction to their seeming fear of him, though Addison could tell by the set of Baxter's shoulders that it bothered him. Some GEs took being ignored better than others. Baxter wasn't one of them, not since his injury.

Addison wondered if the surgery the doctors did on Baxter had messed something up inside him, making him more like Trues than the GEs. Addison gave a mental shrug.

He caught Baxter's eye, then nodded toward the door. Baxter lifted his chin before pushing away from the wall to stroll over to meet him there.

"Have you found out where our barracks are?"

"Yes. We're in Barrack A, sir. On the far end of the base."

"As far away from the Trues as they could put us without forcing us off base," Addison muttered.

Baxter shrugged, not seeming to understand why it bothered Addison so much. "Does it matter where they put us? As long as they leave us alone?"

Smiling, Addison slapped Baxter on the back. "You're right, my friend. Let's go get the others and find some food."

"Sounds good to me, sir."

When they got to Barrack A, they found the rest of the unit had already picked out their rooms, leaving Addison and Baxter to share one, which he didn't mind.

He and Baxter dropped off their gear, then he gathered the men and they went to the mess hall. They ate quickly, not wanting to spend any more time than necessary around the other soldiers. No one greeted them or even acknowledged their presence, and Addison's temper was growing.

Baxter seemed to sense how Addison was feeling because he quietly got them all moving back to the barrack. Addison glanced at them as they stood in the hallway.

"You're off duty right now, so you're free to go anywhere you want, as long as you let Baxter know. If we're needed for any missions tonight, Baxter will let you know. Dismissed."

Addison went into their room, then flopped on his bed. He was staring up at the ceiling when Baxter came in. He didn't acknowledge his friend, even though he could hear Baxter moving around, removing his gear and clothes.

"I'm going to take a shower," Baxter informed him quietly.

"That's a good idea. I think I'll take one as well." He sat up and stared at Baxter, who stood just inside the room, towel wrapped around his waist.

While Addison was built with less bulk, Baxter was all

muscle and strength. He stood six-one, three inches taller than Addison, with tan skin and dark eyes and hair. To be honest, there wasn't anything truly remarkable about Baxter. Addison had seen hundreds of men who looked just like him. Depending on their serial number, the GEs either looked like Addison or Baxter, which made it difficult for Trues to tell them apart at times. It was a good thing they wore their names on their uniforms or the Trues would throw a fit.

Yet there was something different about Baxter — something that had caught Addison's eye and hadn't let him go. Maybe it was the spark of intelligence — something he'd never seen in another of the GEs – shining in Baxter's eyes. All the battles they'd been in had left scars on Baxter's body, and maybe Addison shouldn't find them attractive, but he did. They reminded him of all the times Baxter had been there, fighting beside him and saving his hide fight after fight.

"Are you coming with me?" Baxter asked, and Addison blinked, breaking his perusal of Baxter's body.

"Yes." Addison quickly stripped, then grabbed his shower kit and towel. "I hope they have more hot water than the last base we were at."

"I know. It was like bathing in an ice flow at times." Baxter shuddered at the thought.

They went across the hall to the communal showers. Baxter stepped into the first stall, and Addison chose the one next to him. Addison hung his towel on the hook, then turned the water on.

Steam was rising soon afterward, and Addison stepped underneath the cascade of hot liquid. He groaned as the warmth soaked into his muscles, loosening them.

"Feels good, doesn't it?" Baxter asked from the other shower.

"God, yes. I needed this." He glanced over to where he saw Baxter staring at him from over the half wall. "I don't think this assignment's going to be any better for us, Bax. I think we're screwed."

Nodding, Baxter flashed him a quick smile. "You're probably right, sir, but what can we do about it? Being a GE means we're different from the others, and people don't like what's different. Never have. Don't matter if we were created to save them. They'll still hate us because they're afraid we'll take over when everything is said and done."

"You remember what I told you?" Addison wasn't being mean when he asked. Sometimes Baxter didn't remember all the things Addison said to him.

Baxter frowned. "When?"

"The last time you called me sir when we were alone and not on duty." Addison tilted his head as he looked at Baxter, raising his eyebrows.

"Oh, right. Sorry, Addison." Baxter ducked his head under the water, rinsing off the soap.

Addison grunted in happiness. He wanted Baxter to treat him like a friend. He didn't believe in keeping a distance between officers and enlisted men. They all fought the same battles and were risking their lives in the same way. Just because he was an officer didn't mean he was better than the men who served under him.

Baxter turned his shower off then started to dry himself. Addison rinsed quickly since he didn't want to miss seeing Baxter naked. He knew there were some who would think there was something wrong with him. GEs weren't really supposed to form emotional attachments.

He was supposed to do his duty and willingly offer up his life if it meant keeping the UEA from gaining another inch of American soil. Addison would die to keep the rest of them free, but he couldn't be an emotionless robot, killing without caring about others.

After grabbing his towel, he scrubbed it over his hair as he stepped out of his shower stall. He shot a glance over to where Baxter stood, toweling off his own head. Baxter was gloriously naked, and Addison trailed his gaze from Baxter's muscular chest, down his chiseled stomach to where Baxter's cock hung, half hard and thick. It was only a little bigger than Addison's, and Addison licked his lips, wondering what it would feel like in his mouth.

Yet he couldn't approach Baxter, not here and not now. His friend was still struggling to find his footing and figure out where he fit into the world. Addison wished Baxter hadn't been hurt in that battle last year, so Baxter wouldn't have to suffer all the doubt.

"Addison?"

"Hmm..." Blinking, he realized he'd been staring at Baxter's cock. He raised his eyes to meet Baxter's amused gaze. "Sorry. I got thinking about things."

"What kind of things? You were staring pretty hard." Baxter winked, and Addison chuckled.

"Nothing that important, Bax. My mind wandered."

Baxter nodded, reaching out to slap Addison's shoulder, and if it seemed he lingered there a little bit, maybe that was Addison's wishful thinking. Instead of taking his hand away, Baxter traced the scar that ran along the upper right of Addison's chest all the way to his lower left side.

Addison shivered at the heat of Baxter's touch. His cock twitched before starting to fill out. He breathed in Baxter's scent—freshly showered male—wishing he could lean in closer to bury his nose in the triangle of skin at the base of Baxter's throat. He swallowed back a moan as Baxter rubbed his thumb over Addison's nipple.

"Bax," Addison muttered, his voice husky, but he hoped he didn't sound needy.

"Oh, sorry, Addison. I didn't mean nothing by it." Baxter jerked his hand away like he'd been burned. He started to turn away, but Addison grabbed Baxter's arm.

"No, Bax. It's okay." Addison glanced down for a second, then gathered his courage and looked at Baxter. "I liked you touching me."

Baxter stared at him for a minute before a tiny smile tilted up his mouth. "Really?"

"Yeah, but maybe I shouldn't like it as much as I did. And maybe not here." Addison gestured around the empty shower room. "People can come in."

"Oh, right, and we probably shouldn't be doing anything anyway. I mean, you're an officer, and I'm just enlisted." Baxter wrapped one of his towels around his hips before grabbing the other one off the floor.

Addison did the same, then followed Baxter back to their room. After he shut the door, he took Baxter's hand in his, leading his friend to his bed. Addison sat, then tugged Baxter down to join him.

Baxter leaned against Addison, their hands entwined and resting on Addison's thigh. They stared at their fingers and all the differences between them. Baxter's fingers were thicker and shorter, and his skin was slightly darker than Addison's. Addison's slender and elegant fingers didn't look like a warrior's, but they pulled triggers just as well as Baxter's.

"Where does this put us?" Baxter seemed hesitant to ask, and Addison didn't blame him.

"At the moment, I'm not entirely sure where this puts us, Baxter." Addison tightened his grip on Baxter's hand. "All I know is it doesn't matter that you're enlisted and I'm an officer. We're the same in every way except rank. You're my friend, and I'll do anything for you."

Baxter brought their hands up to his head, where he ran their fingers along the scar that marked the place where he was injured. "I know you'll do anything for me. Somehow you managed to convince them to keep me in active duty. I don't know how you did it."

Addison didn't want to talk about it, but not because he'd done anything wrong to get Baxter back in the unit. No, he didn't want to talk about it because he hated thinking about how close he'd come to losing Baxter.

He brushed his lips over Baxter's cheek once before easing

away. "We should go to sleep. We're going to be up early in the morning. I'm pretty sure the captain's going to send us back to Section Eight to do some more recon. Probably expect us to stay out there for a couple of days to see if we can catch a UEA spy."

Baxter frowned but didn't argue. He squeezed Addison's hand quickly before letting go to stand up. They both set out their uniforms and guns. Their boots went beside the beds. Addison slid on his boxers, then stood to stare at the beds.

"We don't have to push them together, if you don't want to," Baxter said, ducking his head, while averting his gaze.

Addison shook his head. "No. We can do that, Bax. We just have to remember to put them back to their original positions when we get up in the morning."

He wasn't worried about anyone coming into their room while they slept. The door would be locked, and no one in his right mind entered a GE's room without knocking and announcing themselves first. Since GEs didn't need the same amount of sleep as Trues did to function well, they slept lightly. It would give them enough time to move the beds back.

"Come on." He studied them again. "Maybe it would be easier just to pull the mattresses off the frames and put them in the middle of the room. We can push the frames up against the walls."

"And one against the door," Baxter suggested, doing as Addison said.

Addison wasn't sure about the one against the door, but he went along with Bax. If it made him sleep easier, then Addison would do just about anything for him. Which was why they were sharing a bed.

From some reason, Baxter actually slept when Addison was in bed with him. So Addison endured the rather painful experience of holding Baxter in his arms—painful because all his body wanted was to bury itself as deep inside Baxter as possible. Of course, Baxter wouldn't complain, but

29

Addison couldn't do it because he felt like he was taking advantage of his friend.

If Baxter were to make a move on Addison, he'd welcome him with open arms. But Baxter had lost some self-confidence because his injury, and Addison had been doing his best to build him up again.

He turned off the lights, then crawled under the blankets. After Baxter had joined him, Addison wrapped his arms around Baxter's waist to bring him closer.

"Go to sleep, Baxter. I'm right here, and you'll be okay."

Baxter brushed a kiss over Addison's chest before settling back to close his eyes. Soon his smooth breathing clued Addison in—his friend had fallen asleep.

Addison stared up at the ceiling and thought about everything leading up to this moment. Before he'd taken the assignment of leading his unit, Addison had always believed what he'd been taught. He'd believed all he was supposed to do was fight against the UEA and do his level best to keep them from gaining any more ground. It was his job to give his life, if necessary, to keep the civilians from getting hurt.

After taking over command of this unit and dealing with Baxter and the other men, Addison was beginning to think that maybe there was more out there for them than what the Trues wanted him to accept.

He understood that his questioning and doubts had marked him as a malcontent, and maybe that was what had Tilton on edge about him. Maybe the captain was worried Addison would sow dissension among the ranks. There was at least one other unit of GEs at Alpha Base, but unless Addison went looking for them, they would never meet.

Addison knew Tilton would keep them apart as best he could, yet Addison planned on finding the other GE unit, if only to check and make sure they were being treated all right.

A knock on the door caused Addison to tense, and Baxter woke.

"What's wrong?"

Addison pressed his finger to his lips, then shook his head. "I'll go check."

He climbed off the mattresses before slipping on a pair of pants. Another knock sounded by the time he'd shoved the bed frame out of the way.

"Just a second." He cracked the door a little before peering around the edge. "Yes?"

"Lieutenant Addison?" An unfamiliar GE stood at attention in the hallway.

"Yes?" Addison repeated, not liking the fact that they were talking out where everyone could hear them. When two GEs who weren't in the same unit were seen conversing, it tended to get the Trues riled about the possibility of a conspiracy. He felt a tap on his shoulder and knew Baxter had put the room mostly back the way they'd found it.

"Am I needed somewhere?"

The young man shook his head. "I need to talk to you."

"All right." Addison stepped back, gesturing for the soldier to come into the room. "You need to be careful coming here. I get the feeling Tilton wouldn't like it if he knew we were talking."

"I know, sir, but my superior officer didn't want to come here on his own. He thought it would be too conspicuous to have two GE commanders meeting." He slid into the room, freezing when he spotted Baxter standing in the corner. "I'm sorry. I didn't know you had company."

"This is Sergeant Baxter, my second in command. Whatever you want to talk about, you can say in front of him." Addison motioned toward one of the beds. "Sit and tell me your name."

"I'm Private Wallace, sir. My lieutenant's name is Brown." Wallace sat on the edge of Baxter's bed.

Addison ran through names of GEs in his mind. Brown was familiar to him, and Addison was glad to know Brown was on the base with him, even if he never saw the man.

"I know Brown." Addison sat across from Wallace, and

Baxter moved to stand behind him. Addison knew Baxter would be able to grab Wallace if the soldier went for him.

Wallace might have been a GE, but he was a newer generation, and the scientists had messed with the mutations again. They'd actually weakened the GEs after Baxter and Addison had been created. The Trues had become paranoid that the GEs were too strong. They feared the GEs would band together and rebel. If that happened, there wasn't much the Trues could do to stop them, except destroy them all, and that would be considered a major setback.

"What did Brown want you to tell me?" Addison didn't want to take too much time getting the information. If the captain found out the GEs were talking with each other, Tilton might send one of the units out to be mowed down as an example.

"He wants you to know Alpha Base isn't the worst place for a GE to be. Tilton might not like us, but so far he hasn't gone out of his way to destroy us." Wallace shrugged. "I don't know what the lieutenant's true feelings are, but I figure he knows what he's talking about. We've never been sent into a situation without backup or anything like that."

Addison snorted. "Of course he doesn't send you out without backup. The scientists would be furious at the waste of money and time killing you would cause. They've spent a lot of effort on crafting us, and they can't get that back."

"Yet we were made to die," Wallace pointed out.

"Yes, but not because some True hates us. We're to be thrown on the sword of the UEA to keep the rest of the civilians and scientists safe." Baxter spoke up from where he stood behind Addison.

"If that's true, why doesn't Tilton want you and Brown talking to each other? For that matter, he doesn't want any of the GEs spending time together unless we're in the same unit," Wallace commented, as he met Baxter's gaze.

Addison wasn't sure he wanted to say anything else to Wallace. It was hell not trusting anyone except Baxter. He bit his lip while wondering whether he should tell Wallace the truth.

"Does he have to have a reason to not want us to talk to each other? He's the commanding officer here at Alpha Base, and his word is law." Baxter stepped up to give Wallace an answer that made sense without Addison having to tell him the entire truth.

Wallace grimaced. "I guess that makes sense. Do you want me to tell Brown anything?"

"Yes. Tell him I got the message. Now, you need to get back to your barracks. I'm not sure what they'll do to you if they find you here." After standing, Addison went to the door.

Wallace joined him. "Don't worry about that, sir. I have a friend here who will cover for me, if anyone asks."

"Really?" Addison shot the soldier a questioning glance. "He has to be a True then, because if he's a GE, it's not going to work."

"Yes, he's a True, and he has the ear of Tilton, so I'm confident I can get back to my barracks without getting in trouble." Wallace shrugged.

"I would be careful with trusting a True, Wallace. You never really know whether you can trust them." Addison held up his hand to stop the protest he knew was coming from the private. "I'm not saying your friend would do that. I'm simply stating you need to be more careful. Anyone could turn someone in to save himself."

"Would you do that? Turn a friend in to save yourself?" Wallace looked between Addison and Baxter.

Addison ignored that question. "Just be careful, Wallace. We already know Tilton is against GEs, and we can't be completely sure how many others feel the same way."

Wallace bit his lip, then nodded. "Makes sense. I'm leaving now, sir. Maybe we'll meet up at some point again."

"Good night, Wallace."

Addison shut the door behind the private, then leaned against it while looking at Baxter. "This whole thing is

33

getting more complicated than I wanted."

Baxter looked puzzled. "I'm not sure what you're talking about."

"Wallace has a friend who is a True, and he believes the man won't turn on him." Addison scrubbed his hand over his hair.

"Maybe he won't. Maybe Wallace is right to trust this guy." Baxter started tugging the mattresses back to the floor.

Chapter Three

Addison didn't say anything after Baxter's comment, and Baxter wondered if he'd said something stupid again. Sometimes when he did, Addison would just let the words dissolve in the air between them. Then he'd start a new conversation on a different topic, and Baxter would forget what he'd said that was stupid.

He never called Baxter on his weirdness. It was almost like Addison didn't notice or didn't care Baxter had changed in any way since last year. Baxter couldn't help but love Addison for that.

"You could be right, Bax. Maybe there's something wrong with me because I can't trust anyone except you." Addison glanced over at him, and Baxter saw the expression on Addison's face.

It was one he'd often seen when Addison didn't think anyone else was looking at him. Sadness and despair haunted Addison's eyes, causing Baxter to fear for Addison.

GEs weren't supposed to feel strong emotions. They weren't supposed to feel love, sadness or fear. Yet Baxter felt all of them, though by far the strongest was love, and it was all for Addison, his commanding officer and his closest friend.

Without thinking, he reached out to cup Addison's face, standing on the mattresses to be able to touch him. Addison blinked, seemingly a little shocked Baxter would do something like that. He pressed his cheek into Baxter's palm, like the feel of Baxter's hand grounded him in a way that nothing else did.

"I think trusting just one person makes you a better person

than most of the Trues I've met in my life. Deep inside, you know I'd never betray you and I'd give my life for you."

Baxter didn't know which of them moved first, but when their lips met, Baxter felt whole for the first time in his entire life. Addison cradled the back of Baxter's head with one hand while encircling his waist with the other. Baxter slid his hand down from Addison's face to grip his shoulder.

He slipped his tongue into Addison's mouth, tasting and testing. Addison's flavor was going to be his favorite from now on, causing Baxter to crave it with every fiber of his being. Addison sucked on his tongue for a second, and Baxter groaned.

Addison eased away from him, then rested his forehead on Baxter's while they caught their breath. "We can't start anything right now, Bax. Not until I know for sure we're safe here. I won't risk you because of lust or need."

Baxter breathed in Addison's air, absorbing it. "I know, but you looked so sad. I wanted to make you feel better."

"You do, Bax. No one can make me feel as good as you do. We just need to be careful. We have no friends...and enemies surround us. All I know for sure at the moment is that we can take a breath and regroup. Tilton won't be sending us out into combat yet. He'll keep us doing recon missions until he think he knows our unit."

"That's a good thing, right?" Baxter wasn't sure if it was or not. He didn't understand all the complicated plans and plots Addison had going on. All he understood was that he had to watch Addison's back.

"Lie down." Addison knelt, and Baxter went with him.

Soon they were curled together under the blankets, wearing boxers instead of being naked like Baxter wanted. He accepted what Addison had said about it not being safe for them to let their guard down yet.

"Yes, for right now, it's a good thing that we're just sent out on recon missions. It'll give us time to assess Tilton. I need to figure out how to talk to Brown as well, without Tilton knowing about it." Addison nuzzled against Baxter's temple.

Baxter closed his eyes, forcing back the pounding headache he had as he tried to soak up the care in Addison's touch. "We should be able to figure something out. We're all pretty smart."

Addison chuckled. "Yes, we are pretty smart, Bax. I'm sure we'll be able to work something out before too long. Now we need to get some rest. Tilton will have another mission for us early in the morning."

"Yes, Addison." Baxter loosened his control, letting the pain from his head wash over him and drag him into darkness.

* * * *

"Bax, wake up."

He heard Addison's voice and grabbed hold of it, allowing the words to help him surface from the pool of fear and blackness he'd been swimming in. He blinked a few times, readjusting to being in the present reality. Baxter was on his back, with Addison leaning over him.

"Was I dreaming?"

Addison nodded. "Yes. Do you remember what it was about?"

Baxter shook his head. He never remembered what he dreamed about in any detail. All he could ever tell Addison was that it was painful and scary. There were people screaming in the distance, though he could never get to them. Mostly because he couldn't see them. In his dreams, he was blind and paralyzed.

Addison brushed a strand of hair off Baxter's forehead before leaning down to place a kiss on the tip of his nose. The gesture caused Baxter to smile. Gentleness and caring weren't attributes GEs were taught at the training compounds, yet Addison always seemed to know how to comfort Baxter after one of his dreams.

"It's all right. The doctors said you'd continue to have

37

these dreams for a while after your injury. It's your mind healing itself." Addison shifted around until they were lying on their sides with Baxter's back pressed against Addison's chest.

"I'm sorry I woke you and that I don't know what I dream about," he apologized.

"Hush. You never have to apologize to me for anything. Nothing you do will ever bother me." Addison kissed the nape of Baxter's neck. "Go back to sleep. I've got you."

Baxter, being the good lover and soldier he was, did as Addison told him.

* * * *

The next morning, Baxter joined the rest of the men in the mess hall. He set his tray down next to Franco before joining them.

"Where's the lieutenant?" Franco asked.

"The captain called him in first thing this morning," Baxter informed the whole unit before he took a bite.

"Means we'll be getting a new mission. Probably back to Section Eight. If it's as dangerous as they say, they won't want to send one of the True units up there," Patterson mumbled under his breath.

They all nodded, knowing he spoke the truth, yet Baxter knew none of them held much resentment about that fact. From the moment they were born—or hatched, Baxter didn't really know for sure how it happened—anyway, they knew from the first moment they could comprehend anything that they were to be the sacrificial lambs. The GEs were sent to the front lines and offered up to the gods of war to keep the True humans safe.

Baxter didn't care where he went or what he did because as long as he was with Addison, he'd be fine. He trusted the men in his unit to watch his back as well.

"Does it really matter where they send us?" Gephardt used his fork to point at Baxter. "We go where they want us, and we fight their battles for them."

Baxter glared at the private. "You need to watch what you're saying, especially around here. We're surrounded by Trues, and most of them would rather we weren't here, even if we're saving them."

He glanced around, glad to see there weren't any soldiers sitting close to him. That didn't surprise him, though. Most soldiers sat as far away from them as they could, almost like they would catch something from them. Which, of course, they couldn't, because the GEs never got sick.

His com buzzed, and he checked it to see Addison wanted them to meet him at the armory. Baxter looked at the others.

"Let's go. Have to meet the lieutenant at the armory." After standing, he grabbed his tray to return it to the kitchen.

The rest of the men followed him out of the mess hall, then they headed to the armory. Baxter's heart skipped a beat when he spotted Addison waiting for them outside the building. Addison had left the room shortly after they woke, and Baxter had worried about that. He'd been afraid someone had noticed Wallace stopping by last night and reported it.

"Here as ordered, sir." Baxter stopped in front of Addison, then saluted.

"Good. I need to talk to you for a moment, Baxter. The rest of you go in and grab your ammunition." Addison motioned to the door of the armory.

"Yes, sir."

Baxter waited until the others vanished into the building before asking, "Are we going back to Eight?"

Addison shook his head. "I wish it would be that easy. Tilton's sending us into the DMZ. He wants us to gather as much recon about the UEA as we can, even if that means we go over into enemy territory."

"How long is this mission supposed to be?" Baxter had already started calculating supplies.

"For three days, though he said he might recall us sooner. You're to go to the intel building and get fitted for

39

a biometric camera. He's not taking any chances we might miss something."

Baxter grimaced. "I hate those things. They screw with my eyesight."

"I know." Addison gripped Baxter's shoulder. "I tried to talk him out of it, but he insisted, and you're the scribe among us. I'm sorry."

"I'll deal." Baxter inhaled. "I guess I'd better get over there."

"I'll grab your stuff, and we'll meet you by the front gate. Going in on foot again. No point in drawing more attention to ourselves." Addison paused like he wanted to say something else, but Baxter could tell what he ended up saying wasn't what he'd originally planned. "Make sure you grab some civilian clothes from the quartermaster. We can't go in wearing our uniforms."

"Yes, sir." Baxter gave Addison a quick salute, then headed off to the intel.

Biometric cameras were inserted into a GE's eye. They recorded everything that happened on a mission, even during the downtime, since, once implanted, they didn't allow their host to sleep. Baxter gritted his teeth. As much as he wanted to protest about being used as basically a tripod for the camera, he knew better. Hell, even Trues had to endure the procedure once in a while, though it never came out once it was implanted in them.

Once the mission was over, intel would remove it from Baxter's eye, and after a few days, his sight would be back to normal. He just hated them because while it was in, he and Addison had to act like brothers-in-arms, not anything more. He wouldn't risk getting Addison in trouble for fraternizing with an enlisted soldier.

"Baxter reporting for biometric implant, sir," he announced when he arrived at the desk of the medical branch of intel.

The man at the desk glanced up and frowned. Was it because Baxter was a GE or had Baxter forgotten some protocol?

"I don't understand why they want you to get it implanted. Just because you're a GE doesn't mean this isn't dangerous," he muttered as he gestured for Baxter to follow him. "It's not like we've been able to run trials on this prototype."

Baxter kept his mouth shut. The doctor might not hate GEs, but that didn't mean he liked them either. But something he said caught Baxter's attention.

"Prototype, sir?"

The man pointed to a chair, and Baxter obeyed his silent command. "Yes. These cameras were recently developed and sent out to the forward bases. They're said to be higher definition in pictures and higher quality in voice recording. Also, they aren't supposed to cause as much damage to the implantee's eye."

"You don't sound convinced." Baxter hated being a guinea pig, just like every other person who'd ever been forced to try something new.

"I just wish they had done some lab work on it, but I guess you're a test subject for them."

Baxter sat, letting the doctor lean the chair back. "Are you saying I'm the only one on this base to get one of these prototypes?"

The doctor took out a needle. "Oh no. There's another GE like you who had one put in earlier today. I also inserted them into a few Trues as well. There's no way of knowing how well it works if you only use GEs."

"Well, I guess that's a bonus in some way." Baxter relaxed. There really wasn't anything he could do about it, so all he could do was be a little happy he wasn't the only one getting the implant.

He felt the poke of the needle, then he slowly drifted away. He wasn't completely out. Baxter could still see all the work the doctor did to his eye. It bothered him, but it would take stronger drugs than the doctor had to put him under.

Ten minutes later, he blinked, trying to adjust his vision. His right eye was still blurry, so he stood still, not wanting to run into anything.

"Just a moment. I need to make sure the camera is up and recording. The blurriness should go away once I get it online."

Baxter tracked the doctor as he strolled over to a bank of computers. As Baxter watched, he punched a few keys, and slowly Baxter's vision corrected itself in his right eye until he could see just fine.

A sharp pain tore through his head, causing him to press his fist to his temple. He bit his inner lip to keep from making a sound. He didn't want the doctor to know he was in pain.

"There'll be some pain for the next twenty-four hours, but it should go away after that. If it doesn't, I need you to let me know. There's no way I can fix it or gather the right kind of information if you aren't telling me how your body is feeling." The doctor didn't even look over at him when he said that.

Baxter grunted, not liking the pain. It came too close to what he'd dealt with after his head injury. It sucked, and he'd sworn never to feel like that again. Yet here he was, being used as a lab rat, and he couldn't say a word against it.

A knock sounded on the door, and the doctor called for the person to come in. After entering, Addison stood at attention until the doctor acknowledged him.

"Yes, Lieutenant?"

"I was wondering if you were done with the sergeant. We need to leave on a mission." Addison didn't look at Baxter, keeping his gaze on the doctor.

The doctor didn't say anything, just pressed some keys before turning to face them. "Yes, the sergeant can go. The camera is working and recording now. Remember, though, if the pain gets worse or doesn't go away after a day or so, come to see me and we'll see how to adjust it."

"It will come out after this mission, won't it?" Baxter had to ask, even if it wasn't his place to question.

"Is that what they told you?" He shook his head. "I wish they'd just send you straight to me instead of telling you that you're getting the implant."

"What are you saying?" Addison spoke up.

Baxter was surprised at the anger he heard in Addison's voice.

"I'm saying the implant is permanent. I can't remove it now, and they wouldn't let me even if I wanted to." Doc frowned. "Though if the pain continues, I will take it out. Any sustained pain means something is wrong with it."

"Is there any way to turn it off?" Baxter clenched his hands, forcing his own anger down. There was nothing he could do about it anymore. The operation had been done.

"Actually, yes. It's something that was built into this new prototype. Some of the Trues complained about a lack of privacy." Doc walked over to Baxter, then poked his temple. "Just apply pressure at this point and the camera will turn off. The audio will cut out as well."

The vision in his right eye went black. He blinked again, hating the loss of depth perception. "So turning it off means I won't be able to see out of my right eye?"

"Right. That's the best they were able to come up with." He shrugged, and the doctor seemed rather disgusted by the whole procedure.

"Well, I guess it's better than nothing," Baxter muttered before pushing the spot to turn his vision back on. "Let's get going, sir."

Addison nodded, but didn't say anything as they made their way down the hallway. They stepped out into the daylight, and Addison put his hand on Baxter's arm.

"Turn that thing off."

Baxter shut the camera down, then turned to look at Addison, left side facing him. They were hidden in the corner of the building, shadows disguising them from prying eyes. Addison cupped the left side of Baxter's face, avoiding the spot to turn the camera back on.

"I'm sorry, Bax. If I had known it was permanent, I wouldn't have allowed you to go."

Baxter covered Addison's hand with his and pressed his palm tighter to his cheek. "I know you would've done all you could to keep this from happening to me, but there's nothing you could do about that. It is what it is, and we'll deal with it the best we can."

Addison didn't hesitate as he leaned forward to brush a quick kiss over Baxter's lips. "I will do all I can to make it easier on you."

"I know, and hey, at least I can turn it off now. Didn't have that the last time I got the camera put in." Baxter tried to find a bright side to being treated like an expendable lab rat.

He wasn't happy about it, yet Baxter had learned not to fixate on the bad things that happened to him. He sometimes thought some molecule in his body had evolved closer to human than the scientists had expected.

Addison took a deep breath then stepped back. "Turn it back on and let's go. We need to get to Eight before dark, then we'll be going out into the DMZ once night falls."

"Yes, sir." Baxter tapped his temple before they headed out to where the rest of the unit waited by the gate.

"All right, men. Gephardt, take point, and I'll bring up the rear. The rest of you take your positions accordingly. Baxter, try to stay in the middle of the group to start with until you get used to the camera."

Nodding, Baxter grabbed his gear. "Thank you for packing this," he said to Markeo.

"No problem, man. It sucks that you have to get the camera installed." Markeo shuddered. "I don't think I'd be able to do that."

"It's worse than you think," Baxter muttered.

Markeo shot him a look, but Baxter shook his head. He'd tell them all later once they'd set up camp and he turned the camera off. The rest of the men needed to know what was

44

going on because they could be next on the experiment list, and they needed to be prepared.

Baxter watched Addison salute the guards at the gate as they headed out. For some reason, Baxter felt the urge to look back when they reached the border between the cleared area in front of the base gates and the closest section of the city.

Glancing back, Baxter noticed four men standing at the entrance, watching them walk away. Every instinct in Baxter's soul told him that wasn't a good thing, and he would mention it to Addison once they were well into their mission.

He turned back, following Synder into Section Two, which was the part of the city closest to the base. It was the safest and held the most civilians, though they didn't see any of them. Most of them stayed hidden when units went out, not wanting to draw attention to themselves.

Baxter didn't blame them—a lot of soldiers didn't care if they bothered or even hurt the civilians. There were quite a few people who hated GEs and swore they were the ones who instigated the problems, but Trues were the ones who caused most of the issues.

"All right. Gather up," Addison ordered, and they all huddled around him.

"We're about to leave Two, and once we step over the line into Three, we need to be on guard. Intel says there are bands of outlaws roving the streets. They're heavily armed and won't hesitate to attack if the odds are in their favor." Addison looked like he wanted to say more, but Baxter figured he wouldn't because of the camera.

"Yes, sir."

"Resume your positions. We don't want to get separated, and we'll stop right before we enter the DMZ. If the sun hasn't set, we'll find a building to hang in until it's dark, then we'll move out again." Addison motioned for them to continue.

They slung their packs over their shoulders, then lifted

their guns before taking off again. Baxter looked from right to left, scanning the area in front of him and making sure the camera caught everything. It was feeding back to Alpha Base, and they were recording all the information for further intel.

Baxter didn't see anything out of the ordinary, but since he'd just arrived at the forward base, he'd never been out in the rest of the ravaged city.

"We're being flanked on the left side," Alves muttered softly.

Everyone grunted in acknowledgment as Baxter slowly turned his head so he could record the movements of the civilians on the next street over. He saw them dodge across the alleyways to the relative cover of the next bombed-out building.

Baxter stumbled when the vision in his right eye blurred, and the next thing he knew, the camera had zoomed in and he could see the faces of the men clearly. Addison grabbed his arm, keeping him from falling to his knees.

"What's wrong, Baxter?"

"The camera zoomed in. I can see their faces, and they're all kids. It doesn't look like they're armed either." He wanted to make sure the guys knew the kids weren't armed.

"All right. We'll keep that in mind as we move. As long as they don't attack us, we'll let them trail along." Addison squeezed Baxter's arm. "Can you walk without help?"

Baxter blinked, and his vision went back to normal. "Yes. The zoom went away."

"Damn." Addison growled, his displeasure obvious in the curse.

He understood why Addison wasn't happy. With the camera's zoom kicking in like that, it meant someone else was controlling the implant, and that sucked because there was a foreign object in his body he couldn't control.

"We need to get going, sir. If we stay still for much longer, we'll be surrounded," Franco pointed out, keeping his gaze outward.

"I'm fine, sir. Let's get moving."

Baxter gripped his rifle tighter, praying to whatever god he could think of that the camera wouldn't screw up his ability to defend himself and the others. If it did, and if it ended causing one of the other men to be harmed in any way, Baxter would tear his eye out himself.

"Pick up the pace," Addison commanded, and Gephardt took off at a run.

It was impossible for the kids to keep up with them as they traversed through the rubble-strewn streets and alleys of the city. Baxter kept his gaze focused ahead of him, trusting that the others would keep their eyes peeled for any danger that might come their way.

Chapter Four

Once they got to the edge of Eight, Patterson found an abandoned building for them to regroup in. The sun was just starting to set as they dropped their packs. Addison sent four of the men out to canvas the area and set up a perimeter. Synder and Franco organized their campsite, while Baxter sank to his knees in a corner out of the way.

Addison glanced over at Baxter, worried as he saw Baxter press his hand to his head.

"Is he going to be okay, sir?" Synder asked, seemingly as concerned about Baxter as Addison was.

"The doctor said he would have headaches for the next twenty-four hours. If they continue after that, we need to get ahold of him. I'm not sure how he can do anything because I'm pretty sure the higher-ups wouldn't let us come back to base for that." Addison shook his head. "We need to watch what we say around him, though."

"Don't worry. The camera is off because I couldn't deal with it anymore." Baxter spoke up from where he crouched.

Addison dropped to his knees, resting his hand on Baxter's shoulder. "Are you all right? Alves has the med kit. I'm sure he could dig out some pills for you."

Baxter shook his head. "I'm fine for now. If it gets worse, I'll tell you. I promise."

"All right. Sit there until you feel better. Don't worry about turning the camera on. We've settled in and won't be moving until after midnight. So we have time for you to rest." Addison squeezed Baxter's shoulder before he stood.

The other men returned. Addison motioned them to gather around him and Baxter. The unit surrounded him, and Addison looked every man in the eye.

"Okay, gentlemen, we have some issues that need to be addressed before we head out into the DMZ." Addison gestured toward Baxter. "Baxter was informed today that the camera they implanted in his eye is there permanently now."

"What the fuck?" Markeo clenched his hands. "That's not fair."

"The doctor said he put the camera in some Trues as well. Also, the other important thing you need to know is that someone else can control it." Baxter looked up, and the others gasped.

Baxter's right eye was black — no iris, pupil or white visible. Addison wanted to punch something — or someone — for doing that to Baxter. What right did anyone have to treat another person like that? Yet the scientists believed they had every right to experiment on Baxter and other GEs.

There was a small touch of spiteful happiness in Addison when he heard some Trues had gotten the implant as well. At least it wasn't all GEs whose lives had been changed without their permission.

"There might be another problem. I didn't want to mention it until I could turn the camera off." Baxter grimaced, closing his eyes. Pain must have been beating in his head.

"Take your time, Baxter. We aren't going anywhere." Gephardt reached out, but stopped short of touching Baxter.

None of the other guys ever touched Baxter. Addison wondered if it had to do with his head injury. There'd been a time shortly after Baxter was wounded when he hadn't been able to deal with anyone touching him. Even Addison hadn't been able to do it, and it had driven him crazy, not being able to offer comfort to his friend.

Addison crouched next to Baxter again, resting his hand on Baxter's leg. "Are you okay?"

Baxter shook his head. "It's like someone is trying to turn the camera back on. But as long as I concentrate, I can keep it off. I hate this, Addison. I hate it with every fiber of my being."

"I hate it as well," Addison admitted.

"We all do. This sucks. Why do they treat us like we're nothing? Like we're not even human?" Franco whirled around, then kicked a rock against the brick wall.

"I've asked myself that so many times, and I can never come up with an answer. So I try not to think about it." Patterson crouched down as well.

The rest followed until they were all sitting cross-legged on the ground, surrounding Baxter.

"What was it you wanted us to know, Baxter?" Addison asked.

"There were four men watching us as we left the base. I think they were going to follow us, but I don't know for sure. All I do know was every instinct I had warned me they weren't a good thing." Baxter leaned to the side, ending up with his head on Addison's shoulder.

His friend must have really been hurting, because Baxter would never have shown any outward display of affection or weakness like that if he wasn't. The men in the unit knew there was a close bond between their lieutenant and their sergeant, but none of them had ever said a word about it. Guess it didn't matter to them as long as they could count on Addison and Baxter.

"Shit. Not only do we have to watch for outlaws, roving bands of kids and UEA soldiers, but now we have to worry about our own soldiers." Alves frowned. "And we have to worry about the camera in Baxter's eye spying on us as well as the world around us."

Addison opened his mouth to point out that it wasn't Baxter's fault, but Baxter tapped his side. He looked down at him, and Baxter shook his head.

"Alves, I've already told myself if this camera causes any problems for the rest of you, I'll remove my eye before I allow any damage to you." Baxter pinched the bridge of his nose. "I didn't ask for this, and I'll be damned if they use it to hurt any of my unit."

Addison gasped. "I won't let you do that. If you take out your eye, you'll be taken to one of the compounds and decommissioned. I won't go through the rest of my life without you by my side."

Baxter smiled at him, but Addison knew Baxter would do what he wanted, and the camera in his eye was dangerous to the rest of the men, he would take his eye out, and nothing Addison said or did would stop him from doing it.

"We have an hour or so until true dark. Baxter, you should rest while you've got the chance. Once we start moving, you're going to be busy recording everything."

He patted Baxter's shoulder then straightened. He gathered the other men with a look, and they moved off while Baxter curled up on his side.

"You can talk among yourselves," Baxter told them. "I'm not turning it back on until we're ready to move out."

"Thanks."

The rest of them gathered moved to the other end of the room, and Addison met each man's gaze, seeing anger in them that matched the rage in his heart.

"This really pisses me off," Franco said, which surprised Addison because Franco rarely spoke up about what he was thinking or feeling. He was very much the silent type.

Yet Addison knew what had happened to Baxter was, for most of them, the straw breaking the camel's back. Being treated like what they thought or felt wasn't important, and the Trues were going to do what they wanted no matter what. There had to be a tipping point when the GEs wouldn't take any more, even if they'd been trained to do so. When that happened, the resulting revolt would be disastrous.

"Why are we always the ones getting used as lab rats? Why don't they keep using the Trues?" Gephardt asked. "Our DNA isn't like theirs, so experimenting on us isn't going to help them learn about how it would affect Trues."

Addison held up his hand before any more was said. "We all feel the same way, trust me. And it's not something I plan on letting go on much longer."

It was time to talk to his men. Baxter would be on his side, so Addison wasn't worried about how Baxter would take the news.

"What I'm about to tell you is only between us. There are some others who are part of this, but it's time to tell you. After I'm done, you'll each get time to think about what you want to do. Just because I'm your superior officer doesn't mean you have to follow me."

"What are you talking about, sir?" Alves looked at him, and Addison had a feeling the private had an idea of what Addison was about to say.

"I'm thinking about leaving."

His bald statement landed in the middle of their group like a bomb going off. All his men stared at him with various expressions of shock on their face, except for Alves, who simply nodded.

"Leave? Are you going to try to get out of the military?" Patterson looked surprised Addison would be considering that.

No GE had ever left the military without being decommissioned and sent away to one of the camps.

Addison shook his head. "Not just the military. I'm getting out of here. As soon as I can work some last-minute things out, I'm going AWOL. I'm done being used as cannon fodder and a lab rat."

He pointed toward Baxter, and the others nodded.

"I'm getting out of here because we weren't meant for this. Not anymore. The first generation of GEs were mere robots in many ways. They had no emotions and didn't care about what went on around them. They did their job without questioning their orders." Addison grimaced. "I don't know if it's just nature's way of dealing with things or if some scientist somewhere decided to play with our DNA strands. We're changing, and have been since our generation was born."

Markeo nodded. "I noticed that. In the compound I

trained at, there were some first and second generations of GEs, and I could see the difference between them and my group. You're right. We are evolving, and I'm not sure the Trues are ready for us to be equal to them."

The others nodded as well.

"What is your plan again? And shouldn't we wait until the sergeant is awake to listen?" Synder spoke up.

"The sergeant's going to do whatever the lieutenant does, Synder. You know that." Gephardt poked Synder in the arm. "There's no point in bothering Baxter at the moment."

"Baxter knows my plans anyway. I don't keep anything from him." Addison glanced over to where Baxter was lying on the ground. "We're taking off. I have a few more things to get ready within another month or so, then it'll be time."

"Do you know where you're going?" Markeo seemed interested.

Addison looked at his men and said, "Yes, I do know where we're going, but I'm not going to tell you. You all need to decide on your own whether you want to come with me or not. If you don't, then not knowing where we're headed will save you in the end."

Franco smiled. "That's understandable, sir. We do have a lot to think about before we find out any more, though I do have a question. Are there other GEs who are going with you?"

"Not necessarily *with* us, but there are others who feel the way I do, and I know they'll be taking steps to leave as well. Whether we all end up in the same place or not, I don't know, but I'm not the only one who has decided enough is enough."

Gephardt snorted. "Of course you aren't. I think most of our fellow GEs feel the same as you. I don't need any time to think. I'm with you, Lieutenant. I'll go with you wherever it is you're heading."

Addison held out his hand and Gephardt shook it. "Thanks. I appreciate it."

"You haven't led us astray yet, sir. I trust you to know what you're doing." Gephardt picked up his rifle. "I'm going out to look around. Make sure no one's gotten close."

"Good. Come back in an hour, and we'll make our plans for going into the DMZ."

The men scattered, and Addison went to sit next to Baxter. He rested his hand on Baxter's back, letting his friend know he was there for him. Baxter rolled over to lay his head in Addison's lap, and Addison no longer cared what the others thought about the relationship between him and Baxter.

Addison stroked his hand over Baxter's hair. "How are you doing?"

"It hurts, but not any worse than my injury last year. I just can't open my eyes because of the way the camera wants to focus in on things without my having any control over it. That's one of the reasons why I turned it off." Baxter huffed.

"Well, once we get moving, you'll have to turn it back on. We can't keep it off for much longer, or they're going to think there's something wrong."

"I think someone followed us from the base, Addison. I'm not entirely convinced we're meant to come back from this mission. Maybe we should think about leaving sooner rather than later." Baxter peered up at Addison through his eyelashes.

"We're not ready. We don't have all the supplies we'll need." Addison thought through all the different things they needed to have secured before they could take off.

Baxter touched Addison's hand, entwining their fingers, then bringing their connected hands to rest on his chest. "I'm not sure we have the time to make everything perfect. We have to leave soon, Addison, and we can't take much more time to get ready."

"I told the guys our plans, and I know Gephardt will go with us if we went today, but I'm not sure about the rest of them."

He didn't want to lead any of those men astray, but he also knew he couldn't live the life the Trues wanted him to live anymore. He couldn't stand seeing Baxter or any other GE being treated like they were mere objects without feelings or thoughts.

"If we wait for that perfect moment, it's not going to come, and we'll be waiting for longer than is safe." Baxter slowly sat up, keeping his eyes closed.

Addison slipped his arm around Baxter's waist, letting him lean against him. Baxter laid his head on Addison's shoulder, and Addison rested his cheek on the top of Baxter's head.

"I guess we'll have to see how this mission goes, and if it looks like you're right and they're coming for us, then we'll leave. The guys can decide on their own whether they want to come with us or not." Addison brushed a kiss over Baxter's forehead. "It's always been about the two of us, Baxter."

"You're right." Baxter nodded, then he sighed.

Addison stood, then offered his hand to Baxter, who took it. He helped Baxter to his feet, and they stared at each other for a moment before Addison turned toward the center of the room.

The other men filtered in one at a time until all eight of them were there. Addison helped Baxter move to join them.

"You should probably turn the camera back on, Baxter. We have to plan our mission, and I'm sure the people back at base will want to know what we're doing."

Baxter tapped his temple, and Addison watched as Baxter's eye went from black to blue. Once it was working again, Baxter nodded at Addison, who glanced around at the others.

They made plans then moved out.

* * * *

Addison glanced at the men gathered around him. They'd found a small clearing about a mile into the DMZ that they'd all decided would be good for a resting area. He

55

looked at Baxter, who nodded at him, letting him know he was okay.

What were they going to do with the camera when it came time to run? He knew Baxter's solution would be to take his eye out, but Addison didn't want that. Not after all the shit Baxter had gone through so far in his life.

Suddenly, Baxter whipped his head around, staring out into the blackness. Addison signaled for the others to stay silent and still, knowing Baxter had seen or heard something. After reaching out, Baxter grabbed ahold of Addison's arm to tug him closer.

Addison shivered when Baxter pressed his lips to his ear, trying to get control of the desire he felt to turn his head enough for their mouths to meet. He focused on what Baxter was saying.

"There's a group of six men moving on our left. I'm not sure if they know we're here yet or not." Baxter barely breathed the words into Addison's ear.

"Can you tell if they're UEA or outlaws? Or could they be on our side?"

Baxter shook his head. "The camera has night vision on it, so I can see them, but I can't see any difference in the clothes they're wearing to say for sure who they are."

Addison nodded then gathered his men in a tight circle to relay the information. "I think our best bet is to move into the underbrush here and stay stationary until we know for sure they've moved on. The sergeant and I will go in the direction of the others to keep an eye on them. I'll signal when I want you to rendezvous with us."

"All right, sir."

At the wave of his hand, his men slowly disappeared into the brush and trees surrounding the clearing. Within a minute, only he and Baxter stood there, but while he couldn't see the others, he knew they were there, keeping a close eye on them. He was glad to know they had his back.

"Are you ready to go?" he said softly to Baxter.

"Yes, sir." Baxter took point since he could see best in the dark, and Addison stayed close to him, not willing to let him out of his sight.

For such big men, they moved silently through the forest, somehow managing not to step on twigs or to break branches. Addison stayed within arm's reach of Baxter, hoping the camera didn't destroy or hamper Baxter's ability to protect himself.

Baxter froze, holding up his hand to warn Addison. He gestured toward their right, and Addison strained to see something, anything that would tell him what Baxter saw. After staring for a minute, he barely made out the shadowy outlines of men walking past. He counted — there were six of them, like Baxter had said.

"They're heavily armed," Baxter whispered into Addison's ear. "They're either UEA or some of ours. I haven't heard of the outlaws being armed like that."

"If they are ours, why are they out here skulking around like that instead of telling us they're here?"

Addison didn't expect Baxter to know the answer, and he feared they were there to hunt them down. He started to move, then Baxter grabbed his arm, holding him still.

Looking in the direction of the men, Addison watched as another group passed by. This bunch was obviously hunting the first one, and Addison decided his unit needed to get out of the way. He didn't want any of his men injured and because he didn't know either squad, he wasn't inclined to help any of them.

"Let's get the others and move somewhere else. I think there's going to be a firefight soon, and I don't want to get caught in the middle of it."

Baxter nodded. "I'll search for a trail around them while you gather the rest of the men."

Addison knew his men were close by, so he clicked on their communication link, giving them the coordinates to find him and Baxter. A click came back, acknowledging his orders.

While he waited, he turned in the direction Baxter had

gone. His friend wasn't too far ahead, so Addison wasn't worried about him getting into trouble. The other men appeared out of the darkness, mere shadows, but Addison knew them.

He gestured in the direction Baxter had taken, signing for Alves to take the end position and to keep his eyes open for anyone following them. Alves nodded.

They moved on, doing everything they could to stay quiet and make as little disturbance in the forest as possible, not wanting to alert either of the other groups to their presence.

As they caught up with Baxter, a gunshot rang out. They drew their own weapons as they circled, somehow managing to put Baxter in the middle because Addison wasn't sure how the camera would affect his aim.

More shots sounded, then shouting as the two groups clashed in hand-to-hand fighting. Addison wanted to know what was going on, but he didn't want to risk any of his men to find out. Suddenly, Baxter pushed through the ring of the unit and disappeared into the night. Addison started to climb to his feet, but Gephardt grabbed his arm to keep him where he was.

"He'll be all right, sir. We can't treat him like he's going to break with the first blow. The sergeant has proven he's tougher than we thought he could ever be," Gephardt reminded Addison.

"I know, but he's still getting used to the camera, and I think someone else can control it once it's on. I'm worried that whoever else can use it might do something to ruin his chance of protecting himself." Addison bit his lip, not wanting to seem like he was giving Baxter special treatment, yet he knew he was.

His men didn't seem to care about the extra attention he gave to Baxter. They understood he wouldn't let it get in the way of their missions, and most of the time he succeeded, but there was something about this mission that bothered him.

Addison glanced at the rest of the men, and they looked

at him, letting him know that whatever he planned to do, they would follow. He took a deep breath and crouched back down. He had to trust in Baxter, knowing his friend wouldn't do anything to get himself killed if he could help it.

"We'll wait here until Baxter returns," he told the others.

"Good idea. We don't want to wander around in the middle of a battle. Let them fight it out among themselves, and we'll work out the logistics of it all in the morning," Synder said.

Nodding, Addison settled along with his men, praying to gods he'd never believed in that Baxter would be all right.

A half hour later, a click on his comm link caught his attention, and he smiled.

"Baxter's all right," he told the others. "He says to head out thirteen klicks to the north, and he'll meet us there."

"The fighting's died down. I wonder who won." Markeo slowly stood with the others, keeping their weapons at the ready.

"I'm sure Baxter will know. He wouldn't have told us to move out if it wasn't safe for us to do so." Addison gestured for his men to head off.

They took up their positions, already knowing who would take point and who would bring up the rear. Addison listened to the clicks on his link, reassured that Baxter was okay and that whoever had been fighting didn't know they were in the DMZ.

"I wonder if anyone will know about this battle, or if it'll get brushed under the rug because it's part of the DMZ. Neither army is supposed to be here," Patterson commented as they snuck through the trees.

Franco snorted. "There are more people dying in this three-mile stretch of land than die in battles, I bet. Both sides fight to keep it uninhabited, but there are people who live here, hiding from both armies."

"True, so we have to try to avoid them as well." Addison sighed, as he trailed behind Synder and Patterson.

"We'll be fine, sir. We're the best unit Tilton has at the base."

Addison accepted that as true and slapped Alves on the shoulder. "Let's go find Baxter and see what we can find out."

Chapter Five

Baxter didn't look around, though he could sense the rest of his unit closing in on him. He held up his hand, gesturing them closer. He studied the scene in front of him. There were bodies strewn around the area, and there was at least one soldier alive.

He waited until Addison was next to him before he said, "There's one still alive."

Addison grunted, and Baxter knew his lieutenant was trying to decide what to do about that. Would going to help the man endanger their own mission, or could they help him without anyone knowing they were there?

"The six men who passed us were all members of the AFF, and the injured guy is one of ours. The others aren't UEA as far as I can tell without going to search the bodies."

"There are rebels who live in the DMZ. They don't pledge allegiance to either side. That might be who the others are." Franco edged closer to the field of battle.

Addison sighed, and Baxter knew what that sound meant. Addison would never leave a wounded man without giving him some kind of aid. Baxter took his med kit out of his pack and, nodding at Addison, eased in the direction of the moaning man.

"Go with him, Markeo," Addison ordered. "The rest of you, go search the bodies. See if you can find any ID or dog tags for the soldiers and anything for the others. Also, grab whatever ammo you can find. No point leaving any behind for anyone else."

Markeo tapped Baxter's shoulder, signaling that he could move, and Baxter accepted the order. He edged carefully toward the injured man, letting Markeo keep an eye out for him.

"Who's there?" the man called.

"I'm Sergeant Baxter from Unit Foxtrot Zulu. We're from Alpha Base on a mission to do recon in the DMZ," Baxter let the man know. "What's your name, soldier?"

"It's Wallace, Sarge."

Baxter dropped to his knees next to Wallace, and, without even thinking, he tapped his temple, shutting off the camera. His right eye went dark, making him blink until he could adjust to vision in one eye. Then he clicked on his flashlight.

"Why are you out here, Wallace?" Baxter put the end of his flashlight between his teeth, then looked over Wallace's body, searching for his wounds.

"Tilton sent our unit out here to do recon of the DMZ. He said the UEA was moving into the area, and he wanted us to find out what we could." Wallace's breath whistled as he spoke, and Baxter didn't like the sound of that.

After he reached over to tap Markeo's arm, he removed the flashlight. "I need another set of hands. Have Addison send Patterson over here."

"Yes, Sarge." Markeo moved off a little bit to contact Addison.

"Did Tilton send us out because he knew we'd end up here and get shot?" Wallace took hold of Baxter's arm, squeezing it tightly.

"I don't know."

"I'm here, Sarge." Patterson dropped to his knees next to Baxter.

"I need you to hold the flashlight while I look for the wound. Wallace, this is Private Patterson. He's a good guy and will be helping me to take care of you."

"All right. All the others? They're dead, aren't they?"

Baxter nodded. "Yes. I'm sorry."

He tore open Wallace's blood-soaked shirt to expose the wound in the left side of Wallace's chest. Patterson shone light into the wound, and Baxter hissed.

"There's nothing you can do to help me, is there?" Wallace gripped Baxter's hand.

Baxter glanced at Patterson then met Wallace's gaze. "I'm sorry, Wallace. The bullet went through your chest and exited your back. It nicked your artery and punctured your lung. I can't fix that, and you're bleeding out."

Wallace's cough was wet, blood spurting from his mouth. Baxter dug through his med kit to pull out a bandage. He tore it open, then used it to wipe off Wallace's face.

"It's all right, sir. We know something like this could happen to us when we get assigned to a unit." Wallace sighed. "Baxter, would you do me a favor?"

"Anything, Wallace." Baxter lifted Wallace's head, then laid it in his lap. He stroked Wallace's face.

"Would you tell my friend that I said goodbye? He was as close to a brother as I would ever have." Wallace's breathing hitched, then he said, "His name is Thomas Billings."

"Thomas Billings. I'll tell him as soon as I get back to the base." Baxter bit his lip. "I'm sorry, Wallace. We should've seen this coming."

"How could you have known we'd get hit by a rebel unit living in the DMZ?" Wallace smiled slightly.

Baxter shook his head. "I don't know why Tilton sent you out, since he sent us out here as well. It doesn't make sense."

Wallace barely shrugged and Baxter could see the life slowly leaving Wallace's eyes. As the other men of Baxter's unit gathered around, Baxter bowed his head over Wallace and prayed the man found some sort of peace in death.

He didn't know if GEs went to heaven or not, not having been created in the natural way, but he had the feeling that the gods wouldn't turn their backs on soldiers who died protecting the people they were created to serve.

"I'm sorry, Baxter, but we need to head out. Someone would've heard the fighting, and I wouldn't doubt they'll be coming to investigate. We need to be far from here when they do." Addison laid his hand on Baxter's shoulder.

"All right. I need to turn the camera on, then tape all the other men's faces. That way, they'll be able to identify all the GEs and maybe get an ID on the other men as well." Baxter wiped his hand over Wallace's face, closing his eyes one last time.

Addison stroked his hand over the back of Baxter's head then stepped away. After standing, Baxter took a deep breath before turning the camera back on. It zoomed in on Wallace's face, and the movement caused Baxter to wince. *God, I'm never going to get used to that.*

As he moved through the clearing, he made sure to look directly at the dead men's faces, even if they were destroyed in some way. He shouldn't be affected by the death around him. He hadn't been bred to care about who lived and who died, but death had always bothered him more than he'd ever let on. Probably only Addison knew how much seeing all this death would affect him, and Baxter was glad it was his friend who knew.

Once he'd finished with all the dead men, he rejoined the rest of his unit, who stood at the edge of the clearing. They'd gathered what they could from the bodies. Addison shot him a glance, and Baxter nodded, not wanting to say anything because he knew it would be taped.

"All right. We need to do some recon and see if we can find an easily defensible place to stay for the next three days. I want you to split up and see what you can find." Addison looked at Baxter. "You know the drill. We need to be far enough away from here that we don't get discovered when people start looking."

"Cover your tracks. We don't want the rebels to find us," Baxter unnecessarily reminded them.

They all waved their hands while melting into the shadows of the forest around them. Baxter turned to Addison.

"Do you want me to go out as well?"

Addison shook his head. "No. You stay here. I don't want you wandering around the DMZ with that camera in your head. It might distract you from watching out for yourself."

Baxter frowned. He didn't like the idea of not doing his job or of being treated like he was fragile. He understood why Addison chose to keep him in one spot, though, and while he hated it, Baxter would do as his superior officer commanded.

He crouched down next to the largest tree, settling in while Addison disappeared into the shadows. Baxter would get a message on his comm link when a place had been found.

After leaning back against the bark, he closed his eyes, trying to ignore the pounding in his head. Maybe he should take a pill to get a handle on it, but more than likely it would knock him out, and he couldn't sleep yet.

So Tilton had sent both GE units out to recon the DMZ. Was that on purpose? Did he know about the rebel factions living in the area that would attack either side? Had he wanted both units to be wiped out?

Baxter rubbed his eyes. Maybe that was why he'd had the doctor implant the camera in Baxter...because he wasn't expecting them to return to base. If that were true, then Tilton was trying to kill them, and Addison might be right about wanting to go AWOL instead of risking their lives for people who didn't care about them.

Oh, Baxter had never really questioned Addison's reasoning behind wanting to leave. He would follow his commanding officer wherever Addison chose to lead him. Even if he didn't care for him as deeply as Baxter could ever or had ever cared for anyone, he trusted Addison.

Addison had never steered him wrong or taken him into situations where they couldn't get out. At least, not on purpose. There were times when their superior officers, who were for the most part Trues, had sent them out into battles or recon missions where the enemy had surrounded them.

They'd done their best to survive, and each time one of their unit was killed, Baxter knew Addison suffered guilt for not being able to protect him. He didn't want to add to Addison's guilt.

When Addison told him it was time to go, Baxter would walk away from the life he'd always known into the uncertainty of what lay ahead. Yet he knew as long as Addison was with him, they would end up all right, or at least go down fighting, because there was no way he'd allow Addison to get hurt either.

He thought about his commanding officer, and he shifted slightly as his cock stiffened. Now wasn't the time to think those things. Baxter pressed his palm against the front of his pants, trying to ease the ache.

Baxter had always been attracted to Addison, even before he really knew what it meant. They joined the unit at the same time—around their eighteenth year. Since they were the newbies, they'd been paired together, and it was the best moment in Baxter's life.

Addison had accepted all of Baxter's quirks and oddities without question. He'd never once treated Baxter like he was weird or defective since his injury, and for that alone, Baxter would follow him to the ends of the earth.

But it was also because from pretty much the first moment Baxter had laid eyes on Addison, a warm feeling had grown inside him. The need to have Addison hold him in his arms at night. The desire to stare into Addison's eyes and know the lieutenant wasn't thinking of anyone else but him.

It had slowly morphed into more wanting and needing. Wishing for time alone so they could talk without worrying about others overhearing them. Most of the time it was Addison talking and Baxter listening. Baxter wasn't much of a thinker at the best of times, and he hadn't been created to think. He was the brawn. Addison was the brains.

Addison, so tall and dark. Perfect in every way, even with the scars marring his body from the various battles they'd been in. There were moments when Baxter had to fight not to fall to his knees in front of Addison and beg him to fuck him.

Though, with Addison, it would be making love.

"Baxter." Addison's voice came over the comm link.

Baxter jerked upright away from the tree, then stood. "Yes, sir."

"We found a cave about seven klicks west of your position. Make your way here. I'll have Alves meet you to guide you in."

"Yes, sir."

He glanced around to get his bearings, unslung his rifle from his back, then headed out. At least Addison hadn't sent someone to get him like he was a child. The whole camera thing had freaked Addison out, and while Baxter understood Addison wanted to take care of him, he really wanted to be treated like everyone else.

Moving his head from side to side, Baxter recorded his journey from the clearing to where Alves found him.

"Hey, Sarge, you ready to call it a night?"

Baxter nodded then turned the camera off. For some reason he really couldn't explain, he didn't want anyone at the base knowing where they were spending the rest of the night. He had a feeling that if they knew, they would send a bombing raid to try to kill them.

Alves stood, quietly waiting for Baxter to adjust to his limited depth perception. When Baxter gestured for Alves to lead the way, the private slipped into the brush off the trail like a snake slithering through the foliage of a rainforest. If Baxter didn't know he was there, he'd never have seen Alves. It was one of the private's talents and had served the unit well.

They moved another eight klicks before Alves shoved aside some branches to reveal the cave entrance.

"Didn't want to give away the actual position. Go on in. I have first watch." Alves grinned before heading back out.

Darkness surrounded Baxter the minute he stepped inside. He fumbled in his pocket before pulling out his flashlight. After turning it on, he moved along the faint trail he saw in the dirt covering the cave floor.

When he turned a corner, there was a large cavern and the rest of his unit sat near the back of it, gathered around a small fire. He turned off the flashlight then walked over to them.

Addison glanced up, relief showing in his eyes.

"Why is your camera off?" Addison asked him instead of what Baxter hoped he'd say.

Baxter slid out of his pack, letting it fall to the ground before he sat. He accepted the MRE that Franco handed him, not really caring what kind of meal it was. He just wanted food at the moment.

"I didn't want anyone to know where we were staying tonight." Baxter shrugged. "Maybe I'm getting paranoid, but I just have this feeling that if Tilton and the others know where we are, they'll do something to get rid of us, like they did with Wallace's group."

"What happened there?" Gephardt spoke up from the other side of the fire.

"Tilton sent them out to do the same thing we are—recon on the DMZ. I think he knew about the rebel forces and decided to kill two birds with one stone. Wallace's unit ran into the rebels. You saw the result of that. Both units are gone." Baxter choked down some of his food, suddenly not hungry after talking about Wallace.

The others frowned, and Addison rubbed his chin. Baxter glanced away, not wanting to think about how Addison's hands felt on his body and how he wanted more than just comfort from Addison.

"Damn," Addison swore as he stood. "I was pretty sure Tilton didn't like GEs, but I never thought he'd go to such lengths to get rid of us."

Baxter watched Addison pace, understanding how Addison felt. It was the same emotions they often had as they moved from base to base, hoping to find some True commanding officer who wanted them around. Not one of them had, so they were transferred a lot.

Of course, GEs didn't have families and the only real connections they formed were with their units, so being sent to another base didn't cause many problems. The only good thing about it was that he got to see different parts of the country, but he wished for a place to call his own.

Maybe someday he'd have that, along with Addison to share it with. Baxter gave himself a mental shake. *As much as I want him to be with me for the rest of our lives, Addison might have other ideas.*

"I hate to say it, but I think we might have to consider leaving sooner than I'd planned." Addison paced, while the rest of the unit watched. "We're not ready, and I don't have all the supplies stashed like I wanted."

"We can't take the chance that the next time Tilton sends us out, we get our asses handed to us. None of us are ready to die, sir," Markeo spoke up.

Addison turned to look at him. "I know that, Markeo, but I also don't want to leave without being somewhat prepared. I know where I want us to go, but getting there is going to take us through enemy territory. Are you ready to spend the next year on the run, hiding from everyone around you?"

Patterson cleared his throat. "Excuse me, sir, but yes, I am. If it means I might have a chance to live my life the way I want instead of being offered up as a sacrifice to the gods of war, then I'm in. No matter how long it takes to get to freedom."

"I'm with Patterson, sir." Markeo gestured toward the other men. "I think we're all with you in this adventure. We're all ready to be more than what they created us to be."

The others nodded as well, and Baxter smiled at Addison when the lieutenant looked at him. Addison had never had to ask Baxter what his decision would be. There wasn't any doubt what he'd do. Where Addison went, so did Baxter, even if it was into the wild.

Chapter Six

Addison appreciated knowing his men would follow him anywhere, but he wasn't sure he could deal with the responsibility of dragging them away from the familiar world they lived in to a place that might end up being more dangerous than serving in the AFF.

"What's the decision, sir?"

He took a deep breath, then exhaled slowly. "All right. We'll go, but not right now. We finish this mission and go back to the base. We do what we can to stockpile some supplies. Within a week, if we're not sent out on any other missions before then, we leave."

"And you know where we're going?" Synder asked.

"Yes, but I don't want to tell any of you yet. In case Tilton gets wind of what we're thinking about doing. If he questions any of you, you won't have anything to say about it."

The rest of the men nodded, but Addison noticed Baxter frowning. What was Baxter thinking, and why didn't he look as excited as the others did about going AWOL? He'd always believed Baxter hated being part of the AFF and longed for a different life.

Panic hit him. What if Baxter had changed his mind? What if the one person Addison could always count on to have his back and be with him forever decided not to go?

"Baxter?" Addison hated the doubt in his voice.

Baxter pressed his hand to his forehead, and Addison wondered if his frown wasn't because of pain instead of disagreeing with Addison.

"I'm sorry, but I need to lie down. If you guys talk about

any plans, please don't do it near me. I have to turn the camera back on, and I don't want Intel to find out what we're thinking about doing."

Addison reached down to help Baxter stand. "I laid my blankets and pack over here. Why don't you lie down and cover up with yours?"

"All right."

Before Addison could turn away, Baxter lifted his hand to touch Addison's cheek. He stared down into Baxter's eyes, trying to ignore the literal blackness of one of them.

Baxter brought their lips together, and Addison rested one of his hands at Baxter's waist. He closed his eyes, absorbing Baxter's warmth and his unique flavor. He'd grown to love how the man tasted and the way his body felt pressed against his during the night.

Addison's cock stiffened, and he groaned into Baxter's mouth. He'd never allowed his control to slip enough to feel desire or lust for Baxter because they'd never really had the time or the place to become physically intimate with each other.

He was discovering that he wanted to sleep with Baxter, to feel the man move under and around him. He'd never thought he'd want someone as desperately as he longed for Baxter, yet he'd never made a move on his friend.

Baxter slid his hand around to the back of Addison's head, holding him still as the kiss deepened. He opened his mouth, allowing Baxter to sweep his tongue in. Addison had always been the one in control of how far things went in their encounters, but he relaxed, allowing Baxter to take the lead.

It wasn't until someone cleared his throat that Addison remembered where they were. He broke off the kiss, then took a step away, letting his hand fall from Baxter's waist. Standing there, he studied Baxter for a moment, liking the flush on the man's cheeks and the slight hitch in his breathing.

"As much as I'd love to take this further," he whispered,

"we can't do it here."

Baxter nodded. "I know, but I didn't want you to think I was having any second doubts about going with you. I'm yours to the end of our lives together, Addison, and nothing's going to keep me from leaving when the time comes."

Addison leaned forward to brush a kiss over Baxter's cheek. "Thank you. Now rest. I don't expect you to take watch tonight. Maybe, if the headache is better, you can do it tomorrow night."

He knew Baxter wouldn't want the other men to think he was getting special treatment or that he couldn't do his job. The rest of the unit didn't think that, but Addison knew Baxter still worried about it.

"All right, sir." Baxter shut his eyes, then tapped his head. When he opened them again, his eyes were normal.

How are we going to deal with the camera? Shaking his head, Addison pushed that problem to the back of his mind, not wanting to deal with it at the moment.

Addison helped Baxter spread out his blankets, then rejoined the others by the fire. They spent the next hour quietly discussing their plans for the next day. Addison wanted to use the cave as a makeshift base. They would spend the next two nights there since it seemed more centrally located between the borders.

They examined the detailed map of the DMZ, and Addison split it into four sections. Two-man units would explore each section. If anything was discovered they deemed important, they were to contact Baxter, and he'd come to record it. He was sending Baxter out with Alves, whom he trusted to keep an eye on Baxter.

"All right. That's how things are going to start out in the morning, but we know that by oh-nine-hundred, we'll be tossing our plans out the window and improvising as we go." After standing, Addison wiped his hands on his thighs then gestured to his men. "Suggest you all try to get what sleep you can. You know the watch order. Sergeant Baxter

72

will take up his usual place tomorrow night. I'm hoping his headache will be gone by then."

"'Night, sir," Markeo said, while he gathered up his rifle to relieve Alves on guard duty.

Addison went back to the far wall of the cavern where Baxter slept. He didn't worry about taking off clothes or boots, being used to sleeping in them. He lifted the edge of the blankets, then slid under them, pressing his chest up against Baxter's back.

"You probably shouldn't do that," Baxter whispered, and Addison knew he was saying that because of the camera being on.

Addison pressed his lips to Baxter's ear, though he wasn't worried about the camera picking up what he had to say. "Are we sure they can hear us as well as see us? Maybe you should turn it off to be on the safe side."

Baxter stiffened for a second, then relaxed. "They can do both, but I assume that's only when the camera is on." Reaching up, Baxter tapped his temple.

"I'm not saying they aren't, and until we know for sure, we'll turn the camera off when we want to talk about something important." Addison drew Baxter closer to him, rubbing his cock against the man's firm ass.

"Sir." Baxter moaned.

"If I had my way, Baxter, I'd be fucking you right now," Addison admitted.

"Really?"

He couldn't believe Baxter sounded shocked Addison had said that. "You know how I feel about you, but there never seemed to be the right time for anything more than a kiss and holding you during the night."

"Maybe there'll be a moment in the future," Baxter suggested.

"Maybe." Addison brushed a kiss over Baxter's cheek, then said, "Try to get some sleep. We have a lot to do tomorrow."

"All right."

Baxter's breathing evened out, and Addison knew he'd fallen asleep. He lay there, thinking about what the future might hold for all of them once they chose to make a run for it. After that first step toward freedom, there was no going back. His men were looking to him for guidance and leadership, and Addison worried he might not have enough of either of those to give them.

Oh, he knew exactly where they were going, but getting there meant traveling through enemy territory for a long time. Addison knew the odds were against them all making it. He feared they would be captured by the UEA or hunted down by the AFF. Neither side would look kindly on them.

He didn't want to lose any of the men in his unit. Addison considered splitting them up. Giving them directions to a rendezvous point close to the border where he wanted to cross. But if any of them were caught, whoever got them would know where the others would be at a given time on a given day. Addison couldn't risk that happening, especially if it meant putting Baxter in more danger.

Baxter muttered something in his sleep, and Addison tightened his embrace, settling Baxter with his mere presence. Addison looked at him and admitted to himself that he loved Baxter. Probably always had, even though he'd never really thought about it.

What did GEs know about love? They weren't supposed to feel love. Emotions stopped them from being the ultimate killing machines. Addison wondered if something had gone wrong with his and Baxter's generations of GEs.

All those created around the same time as him seemed to be far more evolved than any of the other GEs created before them. There seemed to be more independence, more thinking for themselves instead of blindly accepting orders. They were forming friendships and relationships, where before, individual GEs had never attached themselves to anyone.

There was a time when no GE would ever think about going AWOL. They were dedicated to the AFF's cause and defending the homeland. Now there they were, Addison and his men, calmly discussing abandoning what they'd been produced to do and going in search of a new destiny for themselves.

If they made it to Mexico and beyond, they could lose themselves in the rainforest. There were hundreds of thousands of acres of jungle, and no one would spend any time looking for them. They could live off the land and establish a better place, where they made decisions for themselves without being forced to take orders from men who hated them.

Some of the men might even find women to fall in love with. Maybe they would want to have children. Addison paused in his imaginary world to wonder if GEs could even have children. No one had ever spoken of the genetically altered soldiers being able to procreate. Were they like other mutants born in labs who were sterile because scientists didn't want to risk the indiscriminate spreading of mutated genes?

Or maybe the scientists sterilized them as soon as they were old enough? Of course, they could've done it without the GEs ever knowing about it. There were medical procedures they could do that they'd say were to help in other areas. Addison shook his head. Not that he didn't believe they were capable of doing something like that. He didn't want to fly into a rage, and secret sterilizations would do that to him.

But he started thinking about the fact that there weren't any female GEs, or at least there weren't any who served in the military. Was there some confidential camp where they bred female GEs to do things True females didn't want to do? Or was the AFF's governing body allowing only male GEs to be created because they didn't want to risk the chance of a male and female GE having sex and getting pregnant?

His head began to pound, and Baxter grunted next to him. Addison looked to see Baxter staring at him.

75

"You're thinking too much again," Baxter said, stroking his thumb over Addison's bottom lip. "Do you want to talk about what's bothering you this time?"

Addison shook his head. "Not really. It'll only serve to make me mad, and I can't afford to be angry at the moment."

Baxter nodded. "I get that, but you also can't afford to be driving yourself crazy with whatever kind of thoughts you're having now."

"I know, but sometimes I can't shut my brain off, and there's something about the dark of night that's conducive to thinking." Addison nipped at Baxter's thumb before continuing, "Just wondering if GEs could have babies."

"Really? Why would you want to know that? Are you thinking you want to have a baby?" Baxter frowned. "That's an odd thing to be thinking about right now."

Addison chuckled. "I know, but I started thinking about other things, then my mind wandered to whether or not we could breed. I don't know if there are any female GEs out there. Have you ever seen one?"

Baxter shook his head. "I don't know if we can breed or not, but I do think the scientists probably decided we didn't need any females because they can just create more of us in the lab."

"You're right. I guess I just don't want to believe they might have made them and hidden them away somewhere for reasons I don't want to think about."

He blinked as Baxter wrapped his arms around him then pulled him closer. Addison buried his face in the crook of Baxter's neck, breathing in his familiar scent.

"Am I crazy for wanting to get away from here?" he whispered against Baxter's skin.

"If you're crazy, then so are the rest of us." Baxter smoothed his hand down Addison's back. "We're not robots, Addison. I don't think the scientists, as smart as they are, planned on us evolving. The first generation of GEs didn't question or argue with their orders. We're several generations removed from them, and we've seen what the

76

world could be like for us, if we were given a chance to be more than what they expect us to be."

Addison pressed a kiss to the sensitive skin behind Baxter's ear. "What did I do to end up with you?"

"You were good to me and showed me I should expect more. You didn't treat me like I was an idiot. Addison, you taught me to demand that others treat me as someone just as important as they are." Baxter turned his head slightly to bring their lips together.

Addison slid his hand up to hold the back of Baxter's head, though he was careful not to touch Baxter's temple. He didn't think their superiors would appreciate getting an up-close look at his face while he kissed Baxter.

Their lips met, and Addison closed his eyes, savoring the feel of Baxter's mouth on his. He slipped his tongue in to tease along Baxter's, trying to draw him into playing with him.

Baxter joined in, and they stroked and dueled. Addison pressed Baxter back into their sleeping bags, then wedged himself between Baxter's legs. He rocked their groins together and grunted when he rubbed over the hard evidence of Baxter's desire.

He'd always had the idea Baxter might return his feelings, but he'd never thought the timing was right to do anything about it. And yet again, this wasn't a good time either. They were on a recon mission and planning to go AWOL within the next week or so. He should be thinking about that, not about how Baxter felt in his arms.

Baxter broke their kiss, then moaned. "Addison, we shouldn't be doing this right now."

"I know," Addison admitted as he ground against Baxter again. "I know it's not time, but I need to know you're with me in every way."

Arching his back, Baxter gave Addison something to rub on. "I want that, too, but not when there's an audience."

He froze, having forgotten the other six guys were only a few feet away. Addison let his head drop forward to rest on Baxter's forehead, taking deep breaths to get a hold of his lust.

Easing to his side, he murmured, "I'm sorry, Baxter. I need to get control of myself. But don't think I don't want to make love to you and won't take the first opportunity we get to do so."

Baxter snuggled close to him. "I'm going to hold you to that, Addison. Because I love you, and no matter where we end up in the world, I want to be with you in all ways. Does that sound weak to you?"

Addison shook his head. "No, it doesn't. It sounds perfect to me."

"We need to get some sleep. We have two more days wandering around the DMZ. I want us to find out everything and anything we can because the more information we bring back, the less likely they are to pay attention to us." Baxter rested his hand on Addison's chest over his heart. "I don't want to lose you just when I might get the chance to finally have you."

"You've always had me," Addison informed Baxter. "We're just never in a place where I can show you without someone finding out."

Baxter mumbled something, but Addison couldn't understand him, and he realized Baxter had drifted off. He just tugged him closer, hoping Baxter's headache would be gone in the morning. He hated Baxter being in any kind of pain, but he knew there was nothing he could do to take it away. Except let Baxter sleep and try to keep his hands off him.

"It's all right, sir."

Addison looked over Baxter to see Synder sitting close to them. "Did you hear all of that? And what's all right?"

"We don't care. Hell, we've known what's been going on between you since most of us joined the unit." Synder shrugged. "It's like there's this connection between the two of you, and no distance or anything can break it. I'd like to have a chance at being able to love someone like you and

Baxter love each other."

"You will," Addison reassured Synder softly. "Once we get to where we're going, you'll have the chance to find the one person who'll steal your heart away."

Synder didn't look convinced, but again, it wasn't the time to try to keep morale up.

"Get some sleep, Synder. We're busy the next couple of days, then when we get back to the base, we have a lot of work to do before we make our run." Addison knew they would have to be careful, but as long as they stuck together, they'd get away from the base and be well on their way to being free before anyone noticed.

"Yes, sir."

Addison closed his eyes, burying his nose in Baxter's hair. He listened to the men moving around the cave as he slowly drifted asleep.

* * * *

Three days later, Addison glanced at his men. "It's time to head back to base. We've gotten all the information we need from the DMZ."

They were all dirty and tired from wandering around the edges of the DMZ, while trying to keep from being discovered by the UEA. Addison had had the gut feeling someone had been watching them the entire time. He didn't care as long as they stayed away from his unit.

"All right. You heard the lieutenant, gentlemen. Let's head out." Baxter gestured for Franco to take the lead.

They fell into their customary positions as they made their way back toward Section Eight and the AFF's side of the war. Addison grinned as he heard Baxter poking fun at Patterson.

Baxter's headache had lifted their second day out in the DMZ, and he'd gone back to his usual capable self. Addison still didn't like the idea of that camera being in Baxter's head permanently, but he could deal with it for now.

They would have to figure out something when it was time to leave. He didn't want the AFF to be able to find them. It would endanger their lives and the lives of any who might be convinced to help them along the way.

Addison knew Baxter would suggest that they remove his eye to take the camera out of commission but there was no way Addison would allow Baxter to sacrifice his eyesight for them. Not when there might come a time when he'd need his sight to stay alive.

"I'd like to either be at the base or in friendly territory by nightfall, men," Addison said as they moved along one of the trails through the DMZ they knew had only been used by them and animals.

"We can do that, sir," Gephardt replied from where he walked in front of Baxter.

They'd been hiking for a while, moving as fast as they could through the trees, when Franco lifted his hand, signaling he'd seen or heard something. The rest of them froze, while Addison continued up to where Franco stood just outside a clearing.

"What's up, Franco?" Addison asked softly as he joined the corporal.

"This is where that battle that killed the other GE unit was." Franco motioned toward the empty area. "Where are the bodies?"

Addison peered out from the trees, realizing Franco was right. They'd stayed away from the clearing, not wanting to get caught by any group that might stop by to investigate. The bodies had disappeared.

"Do you think there's anyone around?"

Franco shook his head. "I haven't heard or seen anything since we got here."

"All right. Let's go look around. I want to see if we can find out who took the dead."

Nodding, Franco went first, and the rest followed. Addison explained to each of them what he wanted as they went by. Finally, only Baxter stood next to him.

"What do you think happened?" Baxter brushed his hand over Addison's arm.

Addison shrugged. "I'm not sure, but I don't think it was animals that took off with the bodies. I'd think there would be more evidence left. There's nothing here. No sign of a battle at all."

Baxter swept the clearing with his gaze, letting the camera pick up the scene for the intelligence people back at base. Addison stalked over to where Alves crouched next to a section of flat grass.

"Have you found anything?"

The private pursed his lips. "I guess it would depend on what you consider important. I think the fact there's nothing here is odd. No bullets or bodies. No clues anything happened here, though the grass has been crushed by the dead lying around."

He was right. The only signs something might have happened there were the patches of trampled flora scattered around the clearing. *Who took the bodies? Was it the UEA, the AFF or the rebels who live in the DMZ?*

Would he ever find out? He doubted Tilton had sent men to retrieve the GE unit. He knew the only reason Tilton would retrieve the bodies was so the UEA didn't get a hold of them.

The commanders and scientists of the AFF didn't want the UEA to get their hands on a GE, in case the UEA worked out how the GEs were engineered. As far as Addison was concerned, it was foolish to think the enemy's own scientists hadn't already figured out that process.

They had to have captured at least one GE, and Addison had no illusions that the UEA would have treated him any better than the AFF did their prisoners. A captive GE would be experimented on and dissected to discover all of his secrets. It wouldn't matter if he was alive or dead, he would be treated like a lab rat. Of course, it wouldn't have been anything different from what the GE was used to from the Trues.

"What should we do, sir?" Markeo spoke up from where he stood near the other side of the clearing.

"There's nothing we can do. Let's head out, men. We'll never know what happened here after we left them." Addison gritted his teeth. "I hate the idea of their bodies being desecrated in some way. Both sides of the fight deserved to be buried properly."

"Maybe they were." Baxter joined him with the other men. "We don't know for sure where they went."

Addison shot Baxter a look, and Baxter grinned at him, seemingly able to read Addison's mind about what he thought of his comment.

"All right. It's time to go."

He gathered everyone up and got them moving back toward AFF territory. It was definitely time to get the hell out of the army. They needed to be free, and Addison would take them as far as he could. He hoped it would be to Mexico and freedom.

Chapter Seven

Baxter kept his gaze straight ahead as he entered Tilton's office. He and Addison had received orders to report to the captain the instant they stepped foot on the base. He really wanted to go and lie down somewhere dark for a few hours. He'd marshaled through the last couple of days, but it was all he could do to keep his head up, or not to drop to his knees and throw up.

He'd been in constant battle with whoever ran the camera in his head, unwilling to give up total control. When they were on patrol or recon, he let the invisible person have control, but when it came time to rest, he overrode them and turned it off. He wasn't going to allow them to tape or record anything the men said. Baxter didn't want his unit to think he was on AFF's side. He needed to be with them because they were the only people he trusted to watch his back and keep him safe.

Baxter hoped the other seven men felt the same way about him. He didn't really know what he'd do if they didn't. But he wasn't going to worry about that yet. They had to get through the debrief with Tilton, then see if they could gather some supplies or enough credits to buy stuff as they traveled.

"We were told you wanted to see us, sir," Addison said while they saluted.

Tilton glared at them for a minute before saying, "At ease."

They relaxed slightly, clasping their hands behind their backs and keeping their gazes fixed on a spot behind Tilton's head, though Baxter's vision was blurring every few seconds.

"Give me your report from the DMZ, Lieutenant."

Tilton sat back in his chair, studying them both as Addison began to tell him everything that had happened on their mission. He didn't pass over the firefight between the other GE unit and the rebels, but he didn't talk about Baxter's conversation with Wallace.

Baxter made a mental note to find Wallace's friend, Thomas Billings, and deliver Wallace's final message. Whether Thomas felt the same way Wallace had or not, Baxter wasn't going to break his promise to the dead man.

The GEs had to hang together, whether in life or death. It was the only way they were going to survive in a hostile world that wanted to use them until they died.

His eyelid began to twitch, and it took all of Baxter's restraint not to slam his fist into his face to make it stop. It was driving him crazy.

"Do you have a problem, Sergeant?"

Glancing up, Baxter met Tilton's annoyed gaze.

"Yes, sir. I do. Do I have your permission to go to the infirmary?" Baxter gestured to his eye. "I think the camera is malfunctioning or something."

Tilton stared at him for a moment, probably trying to decide whether Baxter was lying or not. Finally, he nodded. "Go to the intel building. The doctor who implanted it will be there."

"Yes, sir."

He felt bad about leaving Addison alone with Tilton, but he needed something done about his eye, and he knew Addison could handle the captain on his own.

Baxter left the office in a rush, needing to get to the doctor as soon as possible. If he didn't get the camera removed or turned off permanently, he'd be taking it out himself, and that wouldn't be pretty or safe.

Flinging open the intel building door, he called, "I need to see the doctor who installed this camera in my eye."

One of the men sitting at a bank of monitors pointed

toward a door in the back. Baxter stalked through the room, ignoring the way the others practically fell as they tried to get out of his way.

He pushed the door with his foot and burst in. Glancing around, he spotted the doctor. Without noticing anyone else, he shot across the room to grab the doctor's arm.

"You're taking this camera out of my head," he ordered.

Doc looked at him, then waved to the other people. "Get out of the room, and don't worry. I'll be safe. He's not going to do anything to me."

Baxter twisted his hand in Doc's shirt, then jerked him up on his tiptoes. "Don't be too sure about that. My head is killing me, and my eye won't stop twitching."

"I hoped the pain would go away, but it seems like your body is fighting the implant. The other GEs we've put the camera in have accepted it without any problem." Doc studied him.

Baxter shoved the man away from him before he started pacing the floor. He smacked his hand against his temple, wanting to turn the camera off. Only being able to see out of one eye was annoying, but it bothered him far less than the constant pounding of his head and the twitching.

"You have to do something, Doc, or I swear to God, I'm taking my eye out. I'd rather deal with the pain and risk than deal with all this other shit."

He stopped in front of the man and glared at him. The doctor pursed his lips, then nodded.

"I guess I can see about taking it out. We don't usually do that, and it's supposed to be a permanent upgrade, but something tells me you'll resort to drastic measures if I don't." Doc held up his hand when Baxter started to say something. "I can't guarantee you'll keep the sight in that eye, Sergeant."

Baxter shook his head. "I don't care. It needs to be gone. Now."

Doc frowned. "All right. I'll have the operating room prepped. You go let your lieutenant know what's going on.

85

Be back here in twenty minutes. Someone will bring you to the OR."

"Thank you, Doc." Baxter clapped him on the shoulder. "I really don't care what the result is, as long as this camera is out of my head."

The doctor didn't look convinced, but Baxter meant what he said. Hell, if he was willing to take his own eye out, not being able to see out of it forever wasn't really a big deal.

Baxter went back to headquarters, looking for Addison. The lieutenant wasn't there, so he went back to their barracks. When he entered their room, he saw Addison sitting on his bed.

"I'm having the camera removed," he informed him as he approached.

Addison glanced up, and Baxter froze at the rage he saw shining in his eyes. He dropped to the mattress next to Addison.

"What's wrong?"

"I have the men gathering up what food and supplies they can get without anyone noticing." Addison clenched his hands, then rested them on his thighs. "I've had it with the whole thing. I'm done being used as cannon fodder and knowing our lives mean nothing to them."

Baxter reached out to take one of Addison's hands in his. He pried Addison's fingers open, then entwined them with his. Leaning against his friend, Baxter said, "What happened?"

"Tilton didn't care about the other GE unit and what happened to them. He said it's just what happens when soldiers meet the enemy. I think he knew the rebels were out there, and he chose to send both of our units to the DMZ. I think he figured one or both of the units would run into them and probably get wiped out."

Addison gripped his hand, and Baxter gritted his teeth to keep from yelling about how tightly Addison held on.

"All right," he said once he breathed through the pain. "We can sneak out as soon the doctor clears me. I need to get the camera taken care of, Addison. We can't go with it being in my head."

"Is it on now?"

He shot Addison a frown. "Do you really think I'd be having this discussion with you if it was? I turned it off before I came into the room. I knew we were going to have a talk, but I figured it was going to be you trying to talk me out of getting the camera removed."

"Why would I do that?" Addison shook his head. "I know how much it's bothered you since it got put in."

Baxter pursed his lips, not wanting to say anything more, but he couldn't lie or not tell Addison. "The doctor says there's a risk I'll lose the sight in that eye, but it's either he do it or I remove my eye myself. I think his doing it would be safer."

"I would think so." Addison bit his lip, then turned to look at Baxter. "You're willing to trust him."

"It's a chance I have to take, Addison. I can't go with you if I have this thing in my head."

"I'm not leaving you behind." Addison wrapped his arms around Baxter, tugging him as close as he could without Baxter straddling his lap.

"I know that, but I can't take a chance. I refuse to be the reason the Trues find us when we run." Baxter placed his head on Addison's shoulder. "I'd go off on my own if I thought they were tracking us because of me."

Addison shook his head. "No. We'll figure it out if it comes to that. But we'll start with the doctor first. I'll go with you because I don't trust him not to hurt you during the surgery."

Smiling, Baxter nodded as he stood. "All right. I need to get back. The doctor was getting the OR ready."

"He didn't seem to have any doubts about doing it or anything?" Addison asked while they walked out of their room.

"Not really, especially after I told him I'd take my eye out myself if he didn't. The weird thing is he told me the

87

camera couldn't be removed after he put it in. Maybe it's some kind of biological thing that once it's introduced into a body, it starts to assimilate into the muscles and nerves."

Addison growled under his breath. "I can't believe it. Yet another experiment done on us without asking."

"He said they put them in Trues as well as GEs. Maybe they were seeing which ones would adjust quicker. Since the other GEs they might have put it in were in the other units, we'll never know how he dealt with it. I can't very well go and ask about the Trues." Baxter led the way back to the intel building. "Oh, I have to find Billings before we leave."

Markeo strolled toward them and Addison flagged him down. "I need you to go find a True named Billings. When you have him, bring him to the infirmary. Baxter is getting the camera removed, so we'll probably be there after it's done."

"Yes, sir." Markeo saluted, then changed directions to head to the base headquarters.

Baxter trusted Markeo to find Billings without drawing attention to himself. People tended to get suspicious when GEs wanted to see Trues, but Baxter needed to deliver Wallace's message before he left the base. He doubted he would ever get another chance.

They returned to the intel building and, after entering, Baxter told one of the men he was meeting the Dr. Cameron. The man nodded, then led them through another door that opened into a large corridor.

"Go to the third door and knock. The doctor will be there waiting for you."

Baxter and Addison waited until the door shut behind the man before looking at each other. He leaned closer to Addison, pressing his lips to the man's ear.

"I'm getting a bad feeling about this," he whispered.

Addison inclined his head slightly, while reaching down to loosen his handgun in its holster. "If things go sour, I want you to get out of here. Find the others and make your run for it. Don't look back and don't wait for me."

"I'm not leaving you behind, Addison." Baxter pressed a hard kiss to Addison's lips. He removed his gun from its holster, holding it down at his side. "We're in this together, no matter what happens."

Addison nodded before kissing him back. "We'll get through this and then we're getting the hell out of here. I'm not dealing with this shit anymore."

The growl in Addison's voice caused Baxter to shiver. Not in fear, but in a flush of need. He couldn't wait until they were somewhere else and he could get Addison to fuck him. It was all he dreamed about at night, even more than being free of the Trues and the life they led.

"Ready?" Addison bumped him with his shoulder.

"As ready as I'll ever be." Baxter walked down the hallway, knowing Addison would watch his back. He never worried about that.

He kept his eyes moving from side to side, making sure there wasn't any movement from the doorknobs. He figured if there were soldiers or people behind any of those doors, they wouldn't come out until whatever happened got started. He didn't plan to get either of them caught in the crossfire.

"This is the door." Baxter gestured toward where they'd been told the doctor waited.

Addison went to one side of the door, while Baxter plastered his back to the wall on the other side. At Addison's nod, Baxter reached out to wrap his fingers as lightly around the knob as he could, then turned it slowly. Tension filled the space between them while they braced for what was beyond the barrier.

Suddenly, the door was ripped away from Baxter's hand, and he brought his gun up, unwavering in his determination to shoot whoever threatened Addison.

"Get in here now," Dr. Cameron demanded.

Baxter shot Addison a surprised glance. It was like Cameron didn't see the gun at all.

"You need to get in here. I can lock this door, and no one will be getting in. If you want that camera out of your head, then you have to trust me. I'm not looking to hurt you, Sergeant." Cameron shot a quick look down the hall. "But there are people who don't want that camera removed."

"I know that, but I just can't trust you with this like you're my best friend or something, Doc. All I can think of is you killing me on the table, and not being able to stop you." Baxter didn't put his gun away, but he did lower it as he stepped into the room.

"Then your lieutenant will need to keep an eye on me. I know if I were to do anything to you, he'd shoot me where I stand." Cameron gestured toward the operating table.

"Damn right I will. You will tell me step by step what you're doing, and if someone comes through that door while you're operating, your head is the first place a bullet goes," Addison promised as he entered the room as well.

Cameron punched some buttons on a keypad next to the door. They heard the snick as locks rammed home, and something relaxed slightly in Baxter. It really did sound like they would have a hard time getting through that door.

"No one will be able to open the door short of blowing it up with a bomb, and they won't risk that."

Baxter handed his gun to Addison. "You should get a hold of Franco and tell him plans have moved up."

Addison accepted the weapon before walking over to the wall. After lying on the table, Baxter watched as Cameron grabbed a needle from a nearby tray.

"What is that?" He had to ask, not that there was any way he'd know if the doctor was telling the truth or not.

"It's a numbing agent. I'm not going to put you totally under because I don't want your unit to wait until you come out of it before you leave." Cameron met Baxter's glare. "I know you're leaving, Sergeant, and I don't blame you at all for going. There's nothing here for you but death."

He and Addison stared at Cameron, shocked that the doctor really seemed to be speaking the truth.

"Why would you think that? Why work here if you feel that way?" Addison motioned toward Baxter. "Why put shit in people as an experiment then?"

Cameron shrugged. "I know you won't believe me, but I do feel like I'm making a difference. I don't treat just Trues here. I told Tilton the minute I got here that my medical oath forces me to help all the wounded, not just the ones he wants me to save."

He came to stand next to the table by Baxter's head. "This is going to hurt like hell, but I have to numb your ocular nerve. And like I said, I can't guarantee that your sight will return. I haven't removed one of these yet, so I don't know how it has assimilated into your eye and combined with your DNA."

"Are you saying this camera is alive?" Addison sounded horrified.

After taking a deep breath, Baxter nodded, and Cameron eased the syringe into his eyeball. The pain threatened to overwhelm him, but he fought the darkness away. He couldn't pass out. He had to stay awake and aware, just in case something happened and he had to protect Addison.

Within a second or two, the needle was removed and his eye went numb. It was almost like the organ wasn't even there. He couldn't see anything from it, which was probably a good thing, since he did notice Cameron picking up a scalpel off the tray.

"You're fucking sadistic, man." Addison snarled, going pale.

Baxter had the idea Cameron must have been cutting in, but he tried to keep his mind off that. He focused his attention on Addison and let his thoughts wander in the direction of what he wanted Addison to do to him when they were alone.

It wouldn't be until they were relatively safe from the AFF and the UEA, but he could dream until then. He fought the urge to reach down to adjust his erection, wishing he had more room in his uniform.

91

Thinking those thoughts probably wasn't the best thing in the world while lying on his back getting a piece of equipment removed from his eyeball. He settled down, doing his best to relax as Cameron worked. Baxter couldn't close his other eye because it would make him want to shut his right lid, and the doctor was cutting through membrane there.

Baxter didn't want to lose an eyelid along with his sight. If he were brutally honest with himself, he wasn't worried about not getting his eyesight back. He could live without his eye, but he couldn't live without his friends and Addison.

When fingers slipped into his hand and gripped them tight, he managed not to jump. After glancing out of the corner of his eye, Baxter noticed Addison standing close to the table. He was focusing on Cameron, making sure he didn't do anything that would endanger Baxter, even though there was no way of knowing for sure if he was or not.

"I have one more incision to make and the camera will be out, Sergeant. Unfortunately, we won't know about your sight for a couple days while your eye and the optic nerve heal. I'm pretty sure you won't be around for me to check to make sure it's healing well." Cameron spoke, and Baxter met the doctor's gaze.

"Considering the captain and the others are going to be pissed as hell that you removed the camera, you're right, Doc. We're getting our asses out of here as soon as Baxter is ready to move." Addison tightened his grip on Baxter's hand.

"Doc, aren't you going to get in trouble for taking this out?" Baxter knew he shouldn't be talking, but he couldn't help asking.

He felt more than saw the doctor shrug.

"Too late for that concern now. I'll deal with them when they come for me."

"You could come with us."

Addison grunted when Baxter blurted out the comment, and he knew his lover wasn't sure about the idea. All Baxter knew was that he didn't want to leave Cameron behind if he was going to be punished for helping Baxter out.

Cameron shook his head. "No, Sergeant. I'll take my chances here. There's not much they can do to me. My brother is the supreme commander of the AFF, so that makes me pretty untouchable."

This time Addison's grunt was full of surprise. "You're fucking kidding me? The supreme commander's brother works at the most forward base in the country. What the fuck happens if the base is overrun and you're taken prisoner?"

"The same that would happen if they took anyone else prisoner. The AFF doesn't negotiate with the enemy, or terrorists, as they see the UEF."

Baxter didn't understand. "Tilton will get in trouble for punishing you for helping us, but if you're taken captive, your brother won't do anything to help you."

Sighing, Cameron stepped away from the table, then set the scalpel down. "It might seem strange, but those are my brother's priorities. I'm not saying I won't be punished, but he'll be the one to do it, not some peon captain."

Baxter blinked, and there was a streak of pain through his head. He gritted his teeth, but didn't say anything.

"There will be some pain to start with, but that should go away as the incisions heal. I'm hoping your sight will return, Sergeant, but because of the way the camera begins to assimilate into your flesh, it's almost like amputating a limb."

Addison snarled, but Baxter reached out to pat his arm. "Don't. He said it was almost like amputating a limb. I guess that means that, unlike the missing limb, my eye might heal and be just fine."

Cameron nodded. "Right. Now, I think you men need to go. The MPs are going to be coming soon because I couldn't keep them from finding out about this."

"You weren't supposed to take it out, were you?" Baxter asked as he rolled off the table onto his feet. He propped himself up against the edge while he tried to keep from passing out.

"No, I wasn't. From what I've been able to figure out, Tilton thinks you're going to try to take over the base. He's afraid you and the other GEs are planning a coup." Cameron shook his head. "The very people who created you are starting to get scared about what they've made."

"That must've been why Tilton sent the other GE unit out as well. He was hoping all of us would be wiped out, or if just one of our teams were killed, then he would have less trouble dealing with the other."

"More than likely." The doctor walked over to the table where a monitor sat. He turned it on, then glanced at the screen. "Yet from what you've said, you're going AWOL, not trying to take over anything."

Both Baxter and Addison snorted.

"We don't want to fight the entire AFF and UEA. All we want is the chance to go someplace where they won't know what we are." Addison rested his hand on Baxter's shoulder, and Baxter didn't care what the doctor thought or said. He laid his cheek against Addison's hand, letting his lover's presence ease him back to normal.

Cameron turned to eye them, but there was no expression on his face. Baxter had no idea what the doctor was thinking.

"I'll be honest—it sounds like a dream, and I don't dream anymore. This war won't be over until we've wiped each other out," Cameron muttered, not sounding convinced that they'd find a place of escape.

"I think the same thing about this war, which is why we're leaving. I refuse to risk my life and the lives of the people I care about for a pointless war. Whoever wins this fight wouldn't treat the GEs any better than the other side does." Addison looked at Baxter, then rubbed his thumb along Baxter's jaw line.

Chapter Eight

Cameron cleared his throat, and Addison turned to look at him. The doctor's eyes skated toward the monitor, making Addison face the screen completely.

"Fuck," he cursed, as he saw several soldiers entering the hallway. He keyed his comm that linked only to the other members of the unit. "Markeo?"

"Yes, sir?" Markeo answered him almost instantly.

"Where are you at in gathering supplies?"

"We have enough stored in two Humvees to keep us for a couple of weeks. We'll eventually have to gather new supplies as we go on our way. I'm assuming it's going to take us longer than two weeks to get where we're going."

Addison pursed his lips as he thought, then he grunted. "That's what you've got and what we'll have to take with us."

"Yes, sir. Do you want us to meet you at the intel building?"

The guys would come to break him and Baxter out, but he wasn't sure he was willing to start a pitched battle on enemy ground. "I have to think about it. I don't think it's a good idea to have you drive across the base to shoot us out of here."

"You won't have to. I know of a way we can get you over to the far side of the base without encountering anyone, but we need to leave now." Cameron hurried over to the corner of the room, then shoved a large table out of the way. He threw the rug to the side before opening a trapdoor. "There's a tunnel running under the building. It comes out at the southwest corner of the compound."

Baxter looked at Addison, proving he would do whatever Addison decided. He didn't really have any choice. They needed to get the hell out of there before someone ended up dead.

"Let's go. Markeo, we'll meet you and the others at the southwest corner of the base."

"We'll be there, sir. Take care of yourself and the sergeant." Markeo signed off.

"I'll take the lead," Addison said before Cameron climbed down the stairs.

Baxter was the last one down, and he shut the trap door. There were three slide locks on the underside of the door, which Baxter slid shut. Addison pulled his flashlight out of one of his cargo pockets. Baxter did the same while also removing his gun from its holster.

"Head straight, then when you reach the first fork in the corridor, go to the left." Cameron turned to look at Baxter. "Why did you lock the door? I have to go back up there."

Baxter shook his head, and Addison sighed. He knew what Baxter was about to do. He wasn't inclined to stop him, since he didn't want to leave Cameron behind to face Tilton's wrath. Addison didn't care if the man was the supreme commander's brother.

"We're going to need some leverage to get off the base without anyone being shot, and you're it." Baxter gestured for Cameron to move. "You won't get hurt. At least not by us."

"I know you won't kill me, so what's keeping me from refusing to go with you?" Cameron propped his hands on his hips, glaring at them.

Addison grinned. "You refuse and Baxter tosses you over his shoulder. He'll cart your ass through these tunnels."

Cameron shot Baxter a glance, and Addison chuckled as Baxter nodded.

"I'm a GE, Doctor. I recover quickly, so even though I still don't have any sight in my eye, I can carry you as far as I have to for us to get away from here." Baxter moved to stand closer to the doctor. "You went out on a limb to help me. I'm not going to let you suffer the consequences of those actions."

The doctor inhaled sharply, then whirled around on his heel before stalking away. Addison reached out to swipe his thumb over Baxter's lips.

"Let's go, love. Our lives are about to get interesting, and the dear doctor isn't going to be happy we're dragging him along with us all the way."

Baxter licked the pad of Addison's thumb and smiled when Addison's breathing hitched. "He'll deal with it. Unless there's some way we can drop him on the supreme commander's own doorstep, then he's with us all the way."

"I don't trust the Trues not to kill him and blame it on us."

"Are you two done chatting? I do believe you're going to have most of the base chasing after you in a few minutes, along with my brother."

Cameron's voice drifted down the stone hallway, reminding Addison they had other concerns. He jogged to catch up with the doctor, then took the lead. He would put himself in danger because Baxter and Cameron were vulnerable at the moment.

Once Baxter adjusted to having only one eye, he would take the point as they made their way underground to the edge of the base. Addison trusted that his other men would be where he'd told them to rendezvous. The men in his unit were the best he'd ever served with, and they wouldn't let him down.

Following Cameron's directions, they raced through the tunnels. The doctor stayed with them, and Baxter kept an eye on their back trail.

"How many people know about these corridors?" Addison wanted to know if he should be prepared to meet soldiers coming around the corner in front of him.

"As far as I know, none of the Trues ever discovered these. I know about them because of a GE who used to be stationed here. He would disappear from time to time, then

97

return right before he was declared AWOL. I finally asked him where he went on his little excursions." Cameron shrugged. "He said he found these tunnels while wandering the base one night, and on days when he didn't want to be around people anymore, he'd come down here stay away from them."

"And he just happened to tell you how to find your way through them?" Baxter asked from behind them.

Cameron shook his head. "No, he brought me down here, and we'd spend time walking and talking."

"Why? Why would a True, who happens to be the supreme commander's brother, and a GE spend time together?" Addison couldn't believe it.

"Because he was my brother's lover."

Both Addison and Baxter stopped right where they were and looked at Cameron. Baxter shook his head.

"No shit? The supreme commander has a GE as a boyfriend, and we're still getting treated like dirt. That just doesn't seem right."

Addison had to agree. "Does anyone know about them?"

Cameron snorted. "Of course not. It's not that my brother doesn't want to acknowledge his lover, but you seem to think the AAF is a dictatorship. It's not. He's stuck having to deal with a council of fucktards who can't seem to get it through their heads that the enemy is the UEA and not you guys."

Addison wasn't sure he believed that entirely, but it wasn't the time or the place to argue with the doctor. "We'll discuss this later. We've trusted you this far, though we don't have much choice at this point."

Baxter took the lead this time, and Addison didn't stop him. If Baxter thought he could handle it, then Addison wouldn't question him. He fell in behind both of them, keeping his eyes and ears open to any sound or sign of pursuit.

"Turn left here," Cameron told them when they came to a fork in the tunnel.

Addison watched as Baxter signaled them to halt while he pressed his back to the wall, then slowly inched around the corner. Addison put himself in front of the doctor, though he was pretty sure if they ran into any Trues, Cameron could claim they'd forced him to come and he'd be fine.

In a few seconds, Baxter returned to gesture them to follow. Cameron did, but Addison paused to stand at the intersection and listened. All he could hear was the fading footsteps of his companions.

"Sir? Where are you?" Markeo's voice came over his comm link.

"We're heading your way, Private. Just not where you can see us." He turned to head in the direction Baxter and Cameron had gone.

"Do you have an ETA?" Markeo didn't sound nervous or worried, so Addison wasn't going to hurry and overlook something else that might get them all killed.

He glanced ahead to where Cameron stood. "What do you say, Doc? How much longer do we have?"

Cameron glanced around, obviously getting a sense of where they were and where they needed to go. "I'd say we've got about ten minutes before we get there. We'll be coming out of a small shed right next to the base perimeter."

He relayed what Cameron told him, and Markeo clicked to let him know he'd received the information. He hoped the rest of the unit wasn't drawing too much attention yet.

The Trues on the base might be looking for just him and Baxter, thinking they were the only ones making a break for it, and to be honest, Addison hoped that was what was happening. It would have given the other six men a chance to gather more supplies and ammo.

Addison didn't doubt that it might come to a firefight to get free of the base, but he truly hoped they would make it out because he had a clear idea of where they were headed to begin with.

"Are you sure you don't want to come with us, Doc? We could drop you somewhere once we're out of danger.

I'm sure you could get a ride back to the main base if you wanted to talk to your brother." Addison thought he'd offer, yet he knew Cameron wouldn't take him up on it.

Baxter shot him a quick glance, and he lifted one shoulder in a halfhearted shrug. His friend rolled his eyes, but didn't say what he was thinking out loud. Addison knew what Baxter planned on doing. The doctor was going to be coming with them whether Cameron wanted to or not. Baxter wasn't about to leave him behind to risk being punished.

"I don't think it would be a good idea if I came with you," Cameron said as they continued down the corridor.

"Why not? And don't give me all the bullshit about nothing happening to you here. Hell, Tilton could kill you himself and tell your brother that one of us got off a lucky shot." Baxter stopped in front of a metal ladder leading up toward the ceiling.

Addison decided to let Baxter take the lead on convincing Cameron to go with them. If anyone could do it, it would be Baxter. His friend was very earnest in caring about what happened to Cameron.

"That could happen, but I doubt it." Cameron gestured toward the trapdoor above them. "You need to climb up that, and you should be at the shed right next to the outer wall. Your men should be there waiting for you. Good luck."

"Oh no, we're not leaving you down here." Baxter waved his gun at the doctor. "Now you know I won't shoot you, but I will hit you over the head and carry your ass up this ladder. You're coming with us, Cameron. I don't leave a man behind."

Addison took a step closer to Cameron, ready to grab him if he thought to either run away or take a swing at Baxter. The doctor shook his head.

"I'm not coming with you, but you don't have to worry about me. I'm not going to be around to get in trouble." Sighing, Cameron shoved his hands through his hair. "I've

100

been making my own plans on getting the hell out of here. I just didn't want anyone to know. I've been traveling from base to base, gathering information on the conditions of the camps, plus morale. Not only among the True soldiers, but the GEs as well."

"Holy shit! You're a spy as well as a doctor?" Baxter stared at Cameron.

"Being a doctor makes it easy for me to move around. It gives me a reason to be where I am and talk to everyone." Cameron shook his head. "I can't believe I'm telling you this. You could use this information to get me in serious trouble with Tilton."

"But we wouldn't do that," Baxter assured him.

"I guess I know that, which is why I'm telling you this. While Tilton is chasing after you, I'll be leaving in the opposite direction to get to my brother before the news of you going AWOL does. He needs to know the truth, not what they'll tell him."

Addison scrubbed his hand over his face, then sighed. "All right, Doc. We'll be your distraction, but you'd better get your ass moving to wherever you need to go. While they're going to chase us, we're not going to keep enough of the soldiers busy. They'll be following you eventually, unless you have some people here you trust to watch your back."

Cameron nodded. "I have a few people on base I can take with me. I'll let Billings know we're heading out, and he'll have supplies ready for us."

"Wait." Baxter reached out to grab Cameron's arm. "Is your friend Thomas Billings?"

"Yes. Why do you know him?"

"I didn't, but Wallace, one of the GEs who died a few days ago, was a friend of his. He wanted me to tell him that Wallace said goodbye. He was really adamant about it." Baxter studied Cameron intensely, seeming to want to make Cameron realize how important this message was.

Cameron met Baxter's gaze, then nodded. "I'll let Billings

know. He told me he'd been getting close to one of the GEs on base. I warned him about it since I knew how much Tilton hated and feared you. I was afraid something like what happened to Wallace's unit would happen."

There was nothing to say to Cameron's comment. Too many GEs had been sent out by their True captains to die, which was why Addison was taking his unit and getting the hell off the base. Risking their lives for freedom was a better way to die than being killed because someone higher up in command didn't like them.

"Thank you," Baxter said, not concerned about what Cameron thought or felt as long as the message got to the right person.

A click came over Addison's comm link, letting him know Markeo and the other men were in place. He held out his hand to the doctor.

"Thank you for helping us get this far and removing the camera from Baxter's eye. We owe you."

Cameron shook his head. "Who knows? Maybe I'll come and collect on that favor someday."

"We'll pay up," Addison promised. "Get out of here."

After whirling around, Cameron headed back the way they'd come. Once he'd rounded the corner, Addison turned to look at Baxter. Without conscious thought, he leaned forward to brush his lips over Baxter's. Baxter opened for him without any encouragement.

He slid his hand around the back of Baxter's head, holding him still while he plundered the man's mouth. Addison put all of his love and need into the kiss, hoping Baxter knew what he was trying to say to him.

When they broke apart, chests heaving, Baxter cupped Addison's cheek and said, "We're together in this adventure for as long as you want me."

"I'll want you forever and beyond. We're never going to be apart after this." Addison knew there was no way he'd ever let Baxter out of his sight again.

"All right, then let's do this."

Baxter kept his gun in his hand and climbed up the ladder. There wasn't any lock on the door above him, so he simply started to lift it slowly. They had no way to know whether the shed was empty or not.

Addison watched as Baxter held the door open only a few inches, so he could glance all around the room to make sure no one was there. Finally, Baxter shoved the door up and over before he finished ascending the ladder. Addison followed quickly behind him.

They climbed into the shed, then dashed across the floor to where the door was located on the west side. Baxter took a quick peek out of the window under which he knelt. Looking back at Addison, he nodded.

He touched his link. "Markeo, are you ready to go?"

"Yes, sir. We've got the Humvees and supplies. Are you here?"

"Yes, and we're coming out hot. I don't want to waste time. Get everyone in the vehicles. You drive the second one. I'll drive the first, and Baxter's with me."

Markeo clicked his acknowledgment through the link. Addison glanced over at Baxter, who motioned toward the entrance. He took a deep breath before standing up to grab the doorknob. Making sure his gun was ready, he swung the door open and dashed outside.

Baxter was right behind him, and they piled into the first vehicle. Franco and Synder were in the back seat.

"Good to see you again, sir," Franco said, nodding to both Addison and Baxter. "Got your camera taken out?"

Baxter nodded. "Yes. Now we have to get the hell out of here."

"Yes, sir. We have bogeys coming in on our six. The gate is about three klicks to the left of us. Once you turn left on the other side of the building next to you, head straight. If the gate is down, you can run through it. There's nothing to stop these machines." Markeo's voice was calm as it came over the radio.

"Right. Let's go, men. It's now or never." Addison glanced

over at Baxter. "Hold on, gentlemen."

They braced themselves as he floored the gas pedal. The Humvee shot forward, tearing up the dirt under its wheels. He took a quick look in the rear-view mirror to make sure Markeo was right behind him.

Addison inhaled as they skidded around the corner, and he saw the entrance gate in front of them. There were three soldiers standing before the gate, guns up and drawing a bead on them. Baxter started to lean out of the window to take a shot at them, but Addison thumped him on the arm.

"Don't shoot them. They'll get out of the way, and the glass is bulletproof."

Baxter sat back, then ducked as they continued. Addison saw the moment the enemy soldiers realized he wasn't going to stop. One of the men shoved the guy to his right out of the way, while tackling the guy to his left to save him.

"At least he wasn't stupid enough to stand there and expect me to veer around him," he muttered as they slammed through the gate. Addison cringed at the screeching of metal on metal, but he didn't slow down.

"Markeo, are you still with me?"

"Right on your ass, sir," Patterson replied for him.

"Good. Just keep your eyes on our six. We need to know when they follow us and how many they're sending."

"Yes, sir."

He met Franco's eyes in the rear-view mirror, and the corporal tilted his head toward Baxter. Addison lifted his shoulder slightly. He didn't have time to find out if Baxter's eye was working yet, if he'd lost all use of it or if it was too soon to know. At the moment, it didn't matter.

All he was concerned about was getting them somewhere relatively safe, where they could dump the Humvees then start humping their asses across country to the border. He didn't want to spend any extra time in AFF or UEA territory. Neither side was going to be friendly.

"Sir, we have three vehicles coming up on our six." Alves spoke up over the radio.

"Is there any way you can slow them down? We need to get as close to the DMZ as possible before we ditch these vehicles."

"Sir," Baxter said, as he pointed in front of them.

Addison focused on the road, then swore when he spotted the two trucks heading their direction. "Tilton must've called for reinforcements. Synder, the question is now poised to you. Do we have anything that would clear the road in front of us?"

"Yes, sir," both Synder and Alves answered at the same time.

"Good. Do whatever you have to do to get us clear of this mess."

"What about causalities, sir? Should we avoid causing any?" Alves' question was soft.

Addison grimaced, but he didn't have any choice. "This is war, Alves. They might've been on our side at one time, but now, unfortunately, they're trying to take us captive. We must stay free at any cost."

"Understood, sir."

He jumped a little when the top of their Humvee slid open, and Synder stood on the back seat.

"Brace yourselves," Synder warned, and Baxter and Franco hunkered down.

Addison couldn't do anything except keep driving. If he stopped, Markeo would rear-end them, and that would defeat their chances of getting to the DMZ quickly.

"Three, two, one."

A loud explosion went off above them, and the Humvee shuddered as Synder's grenade launcher propelled one grenade away from them. Synder quickly launched two more, and the rest of them waited to see if Synder's aim was good.

"Bullseye," Franco crowed, as the grenades found their targets.

Both trucks veered to each side as they caught on fire, leaving just enough room for their vehicles to get through.

105

None of the soldiers tried to stop them. Addison heard Baxter whispering a prayer as they passed.

"Patterson, did you make it through?"

There were a few tense moments before Patterson's voice came over the radio. "Yes, sir. No injuries and those bogies on our six have been eliminated."

"Great to know, gentlemen. Now we need to keep on this course. I want to hit the DMZ before Tilton can marshal air support. They can't go into the no-fly zone, and I'm pretty sure once we disappear into that place, he'll let us go."

"So we won't have to worry about the AFF anymore, but we will have to deal with the rebels who use that area as their hideout," Baxter pointed out.

Addison shot a quick glance at his friend. "I know, Baxter, but there's nothing we can do about it. And after we're done sneaking through the DMZ, we'll have to get through the UEA's territory without getting caught."

Baxter chuckled. "We never could take the easy way out of anything, could we, sir?"

"No, but I'm glad you all decided to come with me."

"Like there was any doubt," Franco commented from behind him.

Addison chuckled. "I wasn't going to take any of you for granted, Franco. How was I to know none of you were happy about what was going on?"

"Man, no one in their right mind would be happy with how we're treated every day, and God knows, we're smarter than your average True." Synder sounded like he was sneering.

"They hate us because of that, and yet they made us that way," Baxter muttered.

No one replied, and Addison let the silence fill the inside of the vehicle. He needed to keep his attention ahead while the others trained their gaze on the other sides of the road.

"Who has the map?" he asked about ten minutes later when he got the feeling they were getting close to the DMZ. They'd traveled through a rather rural part around the base, not wanting to go through any town where there might be civilians.

He might feel less guilty about killing soldiers, but he'd have a hard time killing innocent people who'd never asked to be involved in their fight.

"I've got it, sir," Franco said.

He heard the rustle of paper as the corporal unfolded the map. He kept going, knowing it would take a second for Franco to orient himself with the direction.

"All right, sir. There should be a dirt road coming up on your left in about three klicks."

Addison kept his eyes trained on the left side, then spotted the break in the brush marking the other road. He slowed to turn before checking his mirror to make sure Markeo had noticed him slowing.

The second Humvee stuck as close as it could as they traveled down the dirt road that gradually began to narrow to a two-rut track.

"The border for the DMZ is about two klicks ahead, sir."

"Then we get rid of the trucks here." Addison eased the Humvee to a stop.

They piled out of the vehicles. He looked around at the seven men he called friends. They were closer than most brothers.

"This is where it gets even more dangerous and scary, men. We're on our own now. There's no turning back."

"We wouldn't do it even if you offered, sir." Baxter held his rifle at his chest. "We're with you every step of the way, Addison."

They all nodded, and he nodded back.

"Then let's do this."

He turned his back on the people who'd created him and took his first step to an uncertain future. But as long as his men had his six, he would be fine.

Chapter Nine

Three hours later, they stopped to rest. They'd been slowly working their way southwest along a faint trail through the DMZ. Baxter didn't say anything while they settled down in a semicircle, each facing out instead of looking at one another. It was standard procedure in enemy territory.

Yet Baxter found himself in the middle of the circle, and he knew it was because none of them were sure about his eyesight. Baxter wished he could tell the rest of the guys he was fine, but it wouldn't be the truth.

He'd hoped the sight would return to his right eye, but so far nothing had changed. It was still dark, and he had the feeling it wasn't going to come back any time soon. So he'd have to adjust.

Thank the gods that as a GE, his body was built to adapt, so he wouldn't lose any real ability to see. The sight in his left eye would get better, along with his hearing and his reflexes. It would just take time for his body to begin the process. He hoped it wouldn't take too long because the closer they got to the border between the UEA's territory and Mexico, the more dangerous it would be.

Mexico patrolled their border with focused violence. No one was allowed to cross over. If you were discovered trying to sneak into Mexico, you were killed, no matter who you were or the reasons why you wanted to be there.

Baxter wasn't planning to lose his life or to let any of the others die either. He assumed Addison had a plan to get them into Mexico without a problem. His lieutenant wouldn't leave that most crucial thing to chance.

"All right, gentlemen." Addison spoke in a low voice,

obviously not wanting anyone to overhear them, though Baxter didn't think anyone was out in the DMZ at the moment. "We need to find a place to spend the night. It has to be easily defendable and hard to find. I don't want the rebels catching our asses just when we got away from the Trues."

"Yes, sir," everyone said.

"Are we ready to go?"

They rose as a unit, each man's gaze pinned on his section of the woods. Alves took the point, and they strung out behind him, knowing their position in the team, with Addison bringing up the end.

Baxter gestured for Patterson to go ahead of him, leaving him right next to Addison. "Sir," he said softly, while glancing at Addison, not wanting the others to overhear him.

"Yes, Baxter." Addison met his gaze before letting it slide back to the landscape around them.

"I still can't see out of my right eye. I wanted to let you know. I don't think it'll be coming back." Baxter shifted his rifle in his hands, not happy with the blind spot.

Addison exhaled slowly, then said, "Cameron warned us it might not return. But it's only been a few hours. We'll see what it's like tomorrow morning after you've slept. The optic nerve needs time to heal, so it just might take a while."

Addison always tried to find the bright side of everything for Baxter. He appreciated that his friend cared that much for him, that he would do or say anything to keep Baxter from falling into depression. It hadn't worked at first after Baxter's head injury last year.

Baxter had been so disoriented and unsure of everything while in the hospital recovering from his wounds. He hadn't known anything or anyone except Addison, and he'd clung to the man shamelessly. Addison had never walked away or complained. He'd sat next to Baxter, talking to him about everything, doing his best to get Baxter back to the way he'd been before the injury.

If Addison hadn't done his best, Baxter would've been reassigned to a rear base where he'd have been put to work on menial jobs until he got too old to work. Then he'd be terminated. Baxter hadn't been ready for that either. Not without having ever known what it was like to be loved by Addison.

Looking forward to that moment was all that had got him through his rehab and rejoining the unit. He'd known that at some point they would have time together without worrying about anyone else finding them. Then Addison would make Baxter his in the most carnal way possible. Hell, Addison already knew Baxter was his man, heart and soul.

It was time for his body to be Addison's as well, yet Baxter understood they needed to get to a safe place before it could happen. Addison would never risk the mission by losing sight of the ultimate goal, and Baxter wouldn't allow that to happen either.

They'd been walking for another three hours, and the sun was starting to set when the word came down through the line that Alves had found an abandoned barn that would work for their night base.

"All right. Lead us there, Alves. We'll set up the perimeter, then get a fire going," Addison commanded.

Baxter jumped slightly when Addison brushed his fingers over his shoulder. Glancing back, he saw Addison smile at him.

"I want to talk with you when we're settled. Have a private chat because we need to get some things straightened out between us."

"Yes, sir." Baxter tensed.

What did they need to straighten out between them? Had he done something wrong without even knowing about it? It was possible because, without Addison to tell him, Baxter had a tendency to say or do things that weren't proper or right.

"Did I do something wrong, sir?" he couldn't help but

ask.

Addison chuckled under his breath, and the sound caused Baxter's cock to stiffen beneath his uniform. "No, honey. You've done everything right, and I think you deserve a little reward for what you've been through."

"A reward?" He mentally winced at the hopeful tone in his voice.

"Yes, Baxter."

The promise in Addison's voice caused a shudder to race through Baxter's body.

They searched the barn, then set up perimeter alarms on each side. After that was done, they started a fire to heat up some food. One of their genetic mutations meant they could function at a higher level on less food than the True soldiers they served with. They would eat tonight, then not have to eat again for at least a week, which should get them out of the DMZ and deep into UEA territory.

Baxter couldn't help glancing over at Addison, anxious to see what Addison had planned for him, but he wasn't going to push it. Addison had to get the unit settled for the night before he could think about himself.

"All right, guys. You know the drill. Figure out who's going to stand watch throughout the night. I'll take last watch." Addison stood, then gestured to Baxter. "You are with me."

"Yes, sir." Baxter joined him. "I can stand watch as well."

"Not tonight. Give your body one full night of sleep so it can adjust to the loss of sight in your eye. Tomorrow night you'll be on watch with the rest of us."

"All right."

He was glad Addison explained why he wasn't on duty tonight. It made him feel better than thinking Addison believed he was compromised in some way and couldn't hold up his position in the unit.

He followed Addison deeper into the barn, where they found a stall with some relatively clean straw covering the floor.

111

"Let's gather some of the hay, then put your sleeping bag over top of it. We'll use mine to cover up with. I think it's going to be a little cool tonight."

Baxter didn't say anything, just did as Addison suggested. Once everything was just the way Addison wanted it, Baxter stared at his commanding officer, trying to figure out what kind of reward Addison was giving him.

Addison stalked up to him, then slid his hand around to cradle the back of Baxter's head. He brought their lips together slowly, almost like he thought Baxter might protest or stop him. There was no way Baxter would stop the kiss from happening. The touch of Addison's lips on his was one thing Baxter had discovered he needed to keep living.

He opened his mouth to Addison, moaning low in his throat when Addison swept his tongue in to stroke it along Baxter's. The light touches drove Baxter crazy, and he pressed himself closer to Addison, absorbing his warmth.

Finally, the kiss broke when Baxter discovered he did need air to breathe. Panting, he stared into Addison's dark, passion-filled gaze. Before he could say anything, Addison dropped to his knees to start fumbling with Baxter's belt and pants.

"Addison?" His voice broke a little on the end of the question.

"Hush, Baxter. Let me do this for you," Addison whispered as he got Baxter's pants open, then started shoving them, along with his underwear, down around his knees.

Baxter gasped as the cool air hit the heated flesh of his cock. Then he groaned when Addison wrapped his mouth around the head. He shivered at the light caress of his lover's tongue, having never felt it on that particular part of his body before.

"Addison, are you sure?" He didn't glance over his shoulder toward where the noise of the others settling down for the night drifted back to them.

Addison let Baxter slide from his mouth, and Baxter missed the heat that had surrounded him. He jumped when

Addison cupped his balls in one hand, then squeezed them gently.

"I'm very sure, Baxter. Today was the first step in our new life, and who knows where this journey will take us. I'm not going to ever pass up an opportunity to love you again." Addison tilted his head in the direction of the other men. "Our brothers-in-arms don't care that we love each other, dear. All they want is the same thing, maybe with another man or with a woman. They all want love like we have."

He ran his fingers through Addison's hair while taking a deep breath. "But I should be the one doing this to you."

Frowning, Addison rocked back on his heels, not letting go of Baxter's cock while doing so. "Why would you think that?"

He hadn't meant to say that, and now he struggled to find the words for what he was thinking. And it was difficult because he knew Addison would argue with him. Finally, he resorted to shrugging.

Addison sighed in exasperation, yet affection gleamed in his eyes as he traced Baxter's features with his gaze. "I know you think you aren't worthy and that I'm some kind of god for loving you. I wish you could see yourself the way I see you, and maybe then you'd understand why I must do this thing for you. And why I don't see it as a chore to get over with as soon as possible."

There was nothing he could say to that, so he pressed his hand to the back of Addison's head, silently asking for what he wanted, even if he didn't think he deserved it.

He shuddered when Addison placed a soft kiss on the tip of his dick before opening to take his entire length in. Baxter didn't apply any more pressure, wanting Addison to move at his own pace, even if it did drive Baxter over the edge with need.

Knees weakening with each suck of Addison's mouth, Baxter reached out with his other hand to grip the top of the stall door. He let his head fall forward, resting his chin on his chest so he could drink his fill of the sight of Addison on his knees in front of him.

It might not have been a position he thought Addison should be in, but if his friend wanted to pleasure him in that way, Baxter wasn't going to argue anymore.

Addison's eyes were closed, but the look of pure joy on his face told Baxter that Addison wasn't doing this just for him. He drew a deep breath as his cock hit the back of Addison's throat. *Christ!* He'd never experienced anything like this.

Of course, he'd never had sex before. Sex hadn't crossed his mind once until he'd realized how much he loved Addison. Baxter had often wondered if he was the one who was deficient in the sex drive area but he'd figured out most GEs were like him.

Maybe it was in their genetic makeup. Maybe the scientists had been trying to weed out any sort of urge to mate, hoping it would keep them under control.

"You're thinking too hard, so I must not be doing something right."

Blinking, Baxter met Addison's gaze, then laughed. "You're doing everything right, Addison."

Addison snorted. "Fine. How about we get naked, then lie down? Kneeling like this is killing my knees."

Baxter wasn't about to say no, so they quickly stripped. Being the soldiers they were, though, they made sure everything was in close reach so they could dress in a hurry, if need be.

He lay on his back, waiting for Addison to crawl between his legs. He was hoping Addison would continue sucking him. But when Addison straddled his head, facing Baxter's groin, he couldn't help but smile.

Now they would both have some fun. While he'd never given anyone a blow job before, he was a fast learner and copied everything Addison was doing to him.

The way his lover moaned made him believe he was doing something right. Baxter grunted when Addison palmed his balls, then squeezed. He found he loved the slight hint of pain. Baxter slid one of his fingers into his mouth alongside Addison's thick cock.

He got it as wet as he could from his saliva, then he ran his finger along Addison's crease to tease his puckered opening. Addison jerked, but didn't pull away. In fact, he rocked back slightly, letting Baxter know he liked what he was doing.

It was a good thing he could multitask or he wouldn't be able to continue sucking Addison while playing with his ass. They moved together, driving each other closer and closer to the edge. Baxter slid two fingers into Addison and twisted them. He hit something inside that caused Addison to shudder like an electric shock went through him.

Once he discovered it, Baxter did his best to hit that same spot every time. After a few minutes, Addison let Baxter's cock slide from his mouth before he rested his cheek on Baxter's thigh.

"I'm going to come if you keep that up," Addison warned him.

Baxter hummed, not wanting to release Addison from his mouth. He didn't care, and he wanted to drink down Addison's cum, to taste the very essence of the man. It wasn't like they could get diseases — GEs were immune to every known human disease and virus.

He sped up, trying to overwhelm Addison so his lover would let go. Addison fucked his face a few more time, then moaned softly as he spilled into Baxter's mouth. Baxter swallowed as much of the hot, bitter cum as he could, but some escaped the sides of his mouth.

After he'd milked the last drops from Addison's cock, he let it slip from his mouth as Addison shifted to straddle his hips. Baxter's shaft was hard and aching. He needed release, but he wasn't going to demand it if Addison didn't feel like helping him. It was okay. He could wait until Addison fell asleep, then finish himself.

Shock rippled through him when Addison grasped Baxter's length in his hand, then slowly impaled his body on it. It was as if everyone in the entire world held their collective breath as Addison's ass eagerly took Baxter in.

Baxter gasped when he was seated as deeply as he could be, and Addison froze, hands braced on Baxter's chest. Baxter met Addison's gaze, and the love shining in Addison's eyes caused Baxter's heart to skip a beat.

There were no words needed between them as Addison began to move, lifting and lowering himself a little faster each time. Baxter arched his hips off the sleeping bag, meeting each slide down with a thrust up. Soon the sounds of skin meeting skin and their low grunts filled the darkness around them.

Right then, it didn't matter to Baxter whether the other men could hear them or not. All he could think about was how tight Addison felt around his dick and how perfect it was to be claiming the man he loved in such a primitive way.

Addison clenched his muscles around Baxter's length, forcing a grunt from him. Baxter gripped Addison's hips, knowing he was leaving bruises, but not caring. If his lover wanted him to loosen his grip, Addison would tell him.

His balls drew closer to his body and his cock swelled as his climax tore through him like bullets fired at close range. Biting his bottom lip to keep from shouting, he flooded Addison with his spunk, thrilled with the idea it was Addison he was claiming.

"Baxter," Addison cried out softly, and a little bit of wetness hit Baxter's stomach as Addison came a second time.

Addison collapsed onto Baxter, and he wrapped his arms around the man. Baxter kissed Addison's sweaty hair before whispering, "Thank you."

"You're welcome, love," Addison replied.

They lay there quietly for a few moments, soaking in the emotions of belonging to each other in every way. For the first time in his entire life, Baxter could say he understood what being the center of someone's world meant, and it was wonderful.

"We should clean up and get dressed," Addison said a minute later.

"Yes, sir." Baxter brushed another kiss over Addison's hair before unwinding his arms to let him sit up.

"What did I tell you about that, Baxter?" Addison shot him a disgruntled look. "How can you call me sir after what we just did?"

Baxter shrugged. "Sorry. Just reflex, I guess."

Addison rolled his eyes, but didn't say anything else as he reached for his pack. Baxter watched as he pulled a cloth from it, then got his canteen out. They washed quickly before they dressed again. Once they had their clothes on, Addison gestured toward their sleeping bags.

"We should try to get some sleep. The last watch comes early."

"I can do guard duty tonight. My brain is adjusting to not being able to see out of my right eye," Baxter informed Addison, but his lieutenant shook his head.

"I want you to rest one full night, then we'll see what the situation is in the morning. Trust me, you'll be pulling your weight on this mission before long. It's just that we're in relatively friendly territory, so I don't need every man on guard for it." Addison knelt, then grabbed Baxter's hand to pull him down next to him.

He stayed quiet while Addison shifted and wiggled them until he seemed happy in their positions. Baxter ended up on his side with Addison wrapped around him, his hand resting on Baxter's stomach.

Sighing softly, Baxter let his eyes close. He hadn't allowed the thought of how much his head ached from having to deal with his blindness while running away from the Trues. His body relaxed into Addison's, loving the warmth and security he felt from just being next to the man.

"I know you're hurting, Baxter. I can read you better than you think, and I know you need to rest. Things will be better tomorrow when you're back to your usual badass self."

Baxter shivered as Addison's breath washed over his neck. "Sorry," he whispered.

"For what? Not telling me?"

He nodded and Addison snorted.

"My love, you don't like to feel like you're a burden to the rest of the men in your unit. I recognize that in you, which is why I accept you the way you are. I'm not mad you didn't tell me you were hurting." Addison nuzzled his neck. "Please, don't hide from me anymore. You and I are a team. Together, we can do anything, as long as we're honest with each other."

"All right." Baxter vowed to tell Addison everything that happened from now on. There was no point in hiding anything when it could end up hurting everyone in the long run.

Addison hummed, which Baxter took as approval. He let his eyes close as exhaustion swept through him. He could count on the others to keep them safe for the night. They didn't have to worry about Trues coming into the DMZ after them, so tonight, the rebels were their main concern.

Baxter listened as Addison's breathing grew heavy and deep. He knew when his lover had fallen asleep because Addison's embrace loosened slightly, though if Baxter had moved, Addison would've kept him there.

The sounds of the others in the front of the barn slowly died away, and Baxter figured they were all either sleeping or had gone out to their positions to keep watch.

What did they think of what he and Addison had done? They had all said they didn't care about their relationship, but was that just because Addison and he were their superior officers? Yet they all had to know neither he nor Addison would punish them if they didn't agree.

Baxter wasn't sure if he should be worried that they might have lied, or just not care about what their opinions truly were. They would be traveling together until they reached wherever in Mexico Addison planned for them to go. After that, who knew what would happen?

Was Addison hoping they would all stay together? What waited for them down in Mexico? Would they be looked down upon because they were GEs, or would it not matter to the people who lived there? He didn't know anything about the countries surrounding theirs. He'd been too busy training to fight to concern himself about geography.

Excitement danced inside him, and Baxter found he couldn't sleep as he began to imagine all the things that could go wrong—and right—as they journeyed to Mexico.

"You're not sleeping," Addison muttered, causing Baxter to jerk.

"I thought you were." He pushed back against Addison's body.

Addison sighed. "I was, but it was almost like I could hear you thinking, you were doing it so hard."

"Sorry."

"What has your brain working overtime instead of resting like I told you to?" Addison rubbed his hand over Baxter's chest before pausing to cover the spot where Baxter's heart beat.

Shrugging, Baxter said, "I was wondering what might be waiting for us in Mexico when we get there. All the good and bad things that could happen along the way."

"Why am I not surprised?" Addison pressed his lips to Baxter's jaw. "There's no point in worrying about it, Baxter. We can't afford to look ahead too far. First thing we have to do is get through the DMZ without running into the rebels, then we have to make it through the UEA forces."

Baxter cleared his throat as desire rushed through him when Addison rocked his erection against Baxter's ass. Could they have sex again? Would Addison want that, even though he'd said they needed to go to sleep? He wiggled his ass, drawing a low moan from Addison.

"Now we've broken that barrier, all I can think about is sinking my cock into your ass and riding you until you shout my name," Addison muttered in his ear.

"Oh!" Baxter trembled, which wasn't a very badass

119

reaction, but he couldn't help it. The thought of having Addison buried deep inside him was all his dreams come true.

He didn't stop Addison from sliding his hand down over his stomach to fumble with the buttons of his pants.

Chapter Ten

Addison pressed his lips against Baxter's shoulder, enjoying how his lover sucked in his stomach to give him more room. They probably shouldn't be doing this again, but Addison couldn't help himself. He'd wanted Baxter from the moment he'd realized he loved the man, and now that he'd had him, he couldn't get enough.

After shoving Baxter's pants down to his knees, Addison dealt with his own. It was hard to focus when Baxter kept rocking back into him, pressing his firm butt against Addison's groin. He practically wept for joy when he freed his cock, but he grabbed Baxter's hips to stop him.

"You need to stop that for a moment, honey, or I'm going to come all over you," he told him.

"And that would be a bad thing?" Baxter's warm chuckle danced along Addison's spine, and he couldn't help smiling at the joy evident in the sound of his lover's voice.

Baxter had never seemed quite as happy since before his injury last year. Maybe he'd been worried about being sent to one of the work camps, or that he'd let Addison down at a crucial moment. Addison hadn't known how much he'd missed the happy Baxter until he saw him again.

"I want to come in your ass, baby." He felt like he was begging, even though he knew Baxter wouldn't deny him.

"I want that as well. I was just teasing you." Baxter pressed back into him again.

Addison encircled his cock to position it at Baxter's opening, then he spit in his palm to coat his length before he pushed in. He took his time, not wanting to hurt Baxter, but he wasn't going to stop until he was buried deep.

When Baxter groaned, Addison stroked his hands along Baxter's sides to soothe him. Once his entire shaft was as far in as it could be, Addison paused, waiting for a signal from his lover that it was okay to continue.

"Are you okay? I'm sorry we don't have any lube," he murmured.

Baxter inhaled, then as he exhaled, Addison felt his muscles relax.

"Yeah, I'm good. You can move now." Baxter clenched his passage around Addison's cock, drawing a grunt from him.

Not taking the time to reply, Addison started thrusting, and he couldn't believe how tight and hot Baxter was. Of course he was going to be tight.

"Oh!" Baxter arched his back, which allowed Addison to slip farther into him. "You feel amazing inside me. You're so big."

Addison's chuckle was slightly breathless. "I love hearing that."

"Pay attention and fuck me, Addison," Baxter demanded, and Addison obeyed.

He drove grunts and moans out of Baxter as he reamed his ass, taking Baxter as fast and hard as he wanted. Addison didn't care what the others were hearing or thinking. All he could think about was claiming Baxter, and even though he knew the rest of the guys in his unit weren't interested in Baxter, he wanted them to know Baxter belonged to him.

Angling Baxter's hips again, Addison nailed his gland, and Baxter cried out. Addison encouraged Baxter to roll over onto his stomach, then helped him to his hands and knees without slipping out of him.

They rocked together, bodies slamming into each other like their entire future depended on them coming at the same time. Baxter moaned, and Addison reached around to grasp Baxter's cock. He formed a tunnel with his fingers, letting Baxter fuck it in rhythm with Addison taking his ass.

"Addison, please."

122

He saw Baxter scrabble at the sleeping bag under him as his climax hit him. Addison bit his lip to keep his own shout from tearing out of his throat. He stroked over Baxter's gland twice before his own orgasm burned his nerve endings.

His cum flooded Baxter's ass, and Addison trembled while trying not to collapse on top of his lover. Baxter didn't have that problem. His elbows buckled and he lay out flat on the sleeping bag.

Addison managed to move his hand out of the way before Baxter landed on it. He sighed when his soft cock slid out of Baxter's ass. He grabbed his T-shirt, then wiped them both off before he tossed it in the corner of the stall. Baxter turned in his arms, snuggling close with a sigh.

"Thank you," Baxter whispered over his skin.

"You're welcome." Addison smoothed his hand over Baxter's head. "I love you, Bax. You know that, right?"

Baxter pressed a kiss to Addison's chest. "I do know that. I've always known you did, even when you didn't say it. You had to have loved me because you stuck by me when no one else did."

Addison nuzzled Baxter's jaw, then kissed him hard. "Go to sleep, honey. Don't worry about things tonight. The rest of us will keep watch, then you can help tomorrow."

Mumbling something Addison couldn't make out, Baxter pushed tighter to him. Addison wrapped his arms around Baxter, keeping him as close as possible.

Things would go back to normal in the morning, and they wouldn't be able to indulge like this every night, even though Addison wished they could. Someday they would be able to spend all day in bed, but not yet.

They had many hundreds of miles to go before they could even think about being safe, but Addison was going to do his best to give Baxter the best night's sleep he could.

After Baxter became a dead weight in his arms, Addison closed his own eyes to try to get some rest before he had to go on watch. But before he could, he felt a presence, though something told him it wasn't anyone dangerous.

Opening his eyes, he saw Markeo standing there. The corporal tilted his head in a 'need to talk to you' gesture. Addison heaved a silent sigh, wishing for one moment that he wasn't in charge and could stay wrapped in Baxter's arms all night.

Wishing didn't amount to a hill of beans when he was the leader of an AWOL band of GE soldiers. He untangled his arms and legs from around Baxter, but before he could climb out of bed, Baxter grabbed a hold of his hand.

"Where are you going?" he mumbled.

"Markeo wants to talk to me." He stroked his free hand over Baxter's head. "Go back to sleep."

Baxter blinked at him. "Do you need me to help out?"

Addison shot Markeo a questioning look, and Markeo shook his head.

"No. I think we can handle this without you right now. If need be, I'll send someone back to get you."

"All right."

Baxter drifted back to sleep, and Addison watched the grimace of pain disappear from Baxter's face. He hadn't realized how much Baxter's head must have been hurting. Being operated on, then having to run for his life, couldn't have helped the situation either.

Addison tugged on his boots before standing. He gestured for Markeo to lead the way back to the front of the barn.

"What's the problem?" He knew something had to have gone wrong for the corporal to come bother them.

When they got to where the others huddled around a small campfire, he noticed that Synder and Patterson were gone. Markeo motioned toward the door.

"I sent Synder and Patterson out for the first watch. They were supposed to check in as soon as they got in position. Well, Patterson did a few minutes ago, but Synder hasn't called in yet."

"Fuck." Addison kept his voice low because he didn't want Baxter knowing there could potentially be a serious problem. "We'll wait another five minutes. Maybe he decided to go farther out to get a better vantage point."

"Yes, sir." Markeo didn't sound convinced, and Addison couldn't blame him.

Every instinct Addison had was tingling, warning him something bad was going on. He didn't want to go off half-cocked, though. They had to give it a sufficient amount of time before they sent anyone out to recon what had happened to Synder.

Addison turned his comm link back on, having turned it off when he'd gone with Baxter. He waited with the others to hear Synder's distinctive clicks over the line, but nothing came.

After the deadline came and went, Addison shook his head. "Someone has to go out and check on him. Did you tell Patterson about Synder not reporting in?"

"Not yet. I wanted to talk to you, then I was going to tell him to head out in the direction Synder went." Markeo was already starting to contact Patterson.

"Fine, but make sure to send someone out to take Patterson's place. We don't want to be caught unawares, in case there's a group of them sneaking around out there." Addison scrubbed his hand over his face. "I should probably go wake Baxter up."

Franco shook his head. "Nah, Lieutenant. We need to let him sleep for as long as we can. He tried to hide it, but even I could tell how much pain he was in. Hopefully, the rest will help him."

"Yeah. At the moment, we don't know what's going on. There could be something wrong with Synder's comm link, or he just hasn't found a spot yet." Gephardt spoke up from where he crouched next to the fire.

Those were plausible possibilities, and though Addison had never heard of a GE's built-in comm link malfunctioning, there was a first time for everything. He didn't know how they were going to fix it, if that was what had really happened. He'd cross that bridge when he came to it.

"Alves, you go relieve Patterson, then tell him to go see if he can find Synder, but make sure he knows to be careful. I don't need anyone else going missing this soon into our journey." Addison propped his hands on his hips. "We'll need to start getting a rescue plan worked out just in case."

"On it, sir." Alves saluted, then grabbed his rifle. He slipped into the darkness beyond the barn door, while Markeo brought Patterson up to speed on what was happening.

Their usual rescue plan wouldn't work in this situation, considering that they had no idea where Synder was or who had him, so they plotted out a basic response until they heard from Patterson.

Finally, Alves called in that he was in position, and told them Patterson had headed out to see if he could find Synder. Addison paced while the others cleaned their rifles and checked over the rest of their gear. Everything needed to be perfect in case they had to make a run for it.

"Franco, go wake up Baxter. If we have to rescue Synder, we're going to have to go in fast and hit 'em hard. And then we might as well just keep going."

Before Franco got up, Baxter spoke from the darkness outside the barn.

"No need to go get me. I'm already up, and you're not going to believe this."

The other men jumped to their feet, rifles pointed at the door where Baxter emerged from the night shadows. Addison relaxed when he saw his lover was okay, but he frowned as he spotted Synder walking behind Baxter.

Then his attention was caught by the squirming figure Synder held by the scruff of the neck.

"I wasn't doing anything," the kid protested.

Synder let go, then gave him a slight shove toward the center of the group. "Tell that to the lieutenant."

"Gephardt, Synder needs his head tended to," Baxter ordered, while staring at the young man standing defiantly

126

in their midst. "This kid tried knocking Synder unconscious. Little did he know the private has a hard head."

"Wait a minute. How did you get outside?" Addison decided that was the most important question to be answered.

Baxter gave him a puzzled glance. "I went out the back."

"Damn. Someone will have to guard back there." Addison stalked over to the stranger. After reaching down, he twisted his hand in the kid's shirt, then tugged him up on his tiptoes. "Who are you and what the hell do you want?"

"I don't have to tell you anything. I'm not part of the military." The kid met Addison's gaze with a narrow-eyed one of his own.

Addison had to hand it to him. He wasn't giving in to the fear that showed deep in his eyes. But Addison knew the kid was afraid. Hell, any smart person would be, especially if he knew they were GE soldiers instead of regular Trues.

"Do you know what we are, boy?" Addison gave him a little shake to emphasize their physical differences.

Their captive's gaze darted among the faces of the men surrounding him, and Addison saw the horrified realization dawn in his eyes. The 'holy shit' moment came when he went limp in Addison's grip.

"Are you going to kill me?" His voice shook.

Baxter snorted. "What's your name, boy?"

"Dash, sir." His gaze didn't leave Addison's face, though he answered Baxter.

"Well, Dash, we don't make a habit of randomly killing people, not even those who attack us first." Baxter touched Addison's arm. "I think you can let go of him, Lieutenant. He's not going anywhere."

Addison did as Baxter suggested, knowing he'd scared the shit out of the kid. Not that he enjoyed doing it, but they needed to know Dash wasn't going to make a break for it—at least not until after they'd got all the information they could out of him.

He motioned at Dash to take a seat near the fire. Turning

127

to look at the others, he saw Gephardt was finishing up treating Synder's wound. "All right, gentlemen. Synder, I want you with Baxter and me. The rest of you finish up eating, then get some rest."

"Yes, sir." Markeo nodded. "I'll let Patterson and Alves know that what's going on."

"Thank you."

After joining Baxter and Synder, he studied Dash again. This time he noticed the young man's raggedy clothes and starvation-thin body. He sat on one of the hay bales then waited while the others found their spots.

Once they were seated, Addison folded his arms over his chest and said, "All right, Dash, I think you need to start talking. You know who—and what—we are. Now I'm pretty sure most of what you've heard about us are lies, but some of it is true."

Dash nodded. "Probably the one where you'd kill me on sight is a lie."

Synder growled then said, "Don't be too sure about that, kid. If you hadn't attacked me from behind, I just might have shot you, then asked questions later."

"Hard to question a dead man," Dash pointed out.

"Who said you'd be dead? You would be dying, though," Synder amended. "And I can get a lot of answers from a dying man."

The glare on Synder's face caused Dash to swallow audibly. Baxter punched Synder in the arm.

"Stop it. There's no need to frighten him even more." Baxter met Dash's gaze.

Dash jerked and Addison figured the kid had just noticed one of Baxter's eyes was completely black. But he had to give Dash credit—he didn't ask what had happened. Of course, he was probably still afraid they were going to torture him or something.

"What were you doing out in the dark, Dash?" Addison asked.

The expression Dash flung his way said Addison was

stupid for asking. "I was searching for food. When I saw him" — Dash waved his hand at Synder — "I thought he looked like he had to have some food on him. So I thought I'd knock him out, clean out his pockets and get away."

"You would've been disappointed," Baxter informed him. "He was standing guard duty. He wouldn't have any food on him."

Addison got Gephardt's attention then gestured to one of the meal pouches he could see sticking out of a pack. Gephardt nodded, letting Addison know he'd prepare it for Dash.

"Where's the rest of your group?"

As much as he was worried about feeding Dash, Addison's first priority was to keep his men safe. He needed to know how many others were out there and whether he needed to send the guys out to round them up.

Dash grimaced, but he seemed to understand lying wouldn't help his cause. "There are four of us. I'm the oldest, so I had Mariah stay with the little ones while I went to see if I could find food for them."

"You're not part of the rebels or of the UEA?" Baxter might not have wanted to scare Dash, but Addison knew he could count on his lover to take a hard stand if they needed it.

Shaking his head, Dash almost fell off his bale from the force of his denial. "No, sir. We're all orphans, and do you know what all the groups in this war do to orphans?"

Addison had to admit he didn't know what became of the children whose parents had died. He'd always assumed they would be taken care of by other families.

"We're rounded up and taken to camps where we're put to work until we either reach our eighteenth birthday and they send us into the military, or we die at some point before that."

The tone of Dash's voice and the look on the kid's face convinced Addison that he was telling the truth. There wasn't any doubt the AFF would do something like that. As far as they were concerned, if there was no family, then there wasn't anyone to argue with how they treated the children.

"Even the rebels?" He clenched his hands at the thought of children being treated that way.

"The rebels are the worst. They don't worry about how old you are. When they get you, they turn you into a soldier. I've seen kids as young as seven carrying rifles and fighting with the enemy."

Addison's heart broke as he imagined the mental and emotional damage a child could sustain from being a soldier at such a young age.

"The UEA does it as well?" Synder sounded shocked.

They might have seen the United European Army as their enemies, yet none of them had ever heard of the UEA treating prisoners badly. Well, unless they were GEs. Rumors abounded of the UEA scientists experimenting on mutated soldiers to learn more about them.

Dash shook his head. "Not so much. They mostly just round us up and put us in camps. If we're from AFF territory, they keep an eye on us in case we're spies. If we're from the DMZ or a rebel camp, they tend to treat us like prisoners of war."

"How do you know this?" Addison was slightly suspicious about how sure Dash sounded about the UEA.

"Mariah and I escaped from a UEA camp last year. We've been living in the DMZ since then. We kind of adopted the little ones a couple of months ago when their parents were killed by rebels." Dash snarled. "Those bastards are no better than the rest of you, for all that they say they're fighting to free us from both sides."

Baxter shifted on the bale next to Addison. "Believe me, Dash. There isn't anyone you can trust in this fight. It's all about power and control. If you can survive on your own, I think you're better off."

Addison frowned, not having expected to hear those words from Baxter. He'd thought his lover would tell the kids to find some adults to take care of them. Yet the more he thought about the situation in the DMZ and anywhere in the two territories beyond the front lines, he realized life was hard everywhere. Most families were having a difficult time feeding their own children. None of them wanted to take on extra mouths to feed.

"That's what Mariah and I thought. It's been hard, and it's going to become harder as food gets even more scarce. Plus, I think there's going to be a shift in the DMZ. The boundary lines are going to move, and where does that leave us?" The teenager shook his head. "I know we should get out of here. Maybe head south to Mexico. I hear they take in refugees once in a while."

Baxter shot Addison a glance and Addison sighed. He knew what Baxter was thinking, and while he wanted to help the kids, he wasn't sure dragging them along with the unit was the best way to do it. It would be easier if they had a vehicle, but he wasn't planning to get one until they got into UEA territory.

"All right. Synder, you go with Dash to get the rest of his group. They might as well stay here in the barn with us."

Gephardt brought over the meal packet, then handed it to Dash.

"Go after he gets done eating. We'll feed them and let them sleep." Addison motioned for them to leave.

Dash eyed him. "Why would you do that for me? Especially considering I was going to steal from your man there." He gestured to Synder with the foil packet.

Addison shrugged. "Maybe because I don't like the thought of kids being on their own and having to worry about soldiers messing with them. Maybe I understand how it feels to be in charge of several lives and not know for sure what's going to happen to all of us."

Baxter bumped his shoulder against Addison, bringing a smile to Addison's face. At least he knew he had Baxter and the rest of his men supporting whatever choices he made. But what if he made the wrong one and someone ended up dying because of it? Addison didn't know if he could live with himself if that happened.

Dash and Synder left, and Addison got the other men arranged around the barn to keep watch. He motioned Baxter to follow him back to the stall where they'd made love earlier. After dropping down onto their sleeping bags, he scrubbed his hand over his face.

"What're we supposed to do now?"

Baxter sat next to him, then rested his hand on Addison's thigh. "We can't leave them without food."

"I know that. We'll make sure they have plenty before we leave, but do we just abandon them to whatever fate has in store for them?" Addison leaned into Baxter's solid body.

"But can we take them with us? We're running, Addison. It's going to be hard enough to get the eight of us across and then through UEA territory, but to get four kids all the way through to Mexico just might be impossible." Baxter's questions were honest and just what Addison needed to hear to help work out his own thoughts.

"I know it could be hard, but don't we have an obligation to help them out the best we can?" Addison covered Baxter's hand with his own. "Don't they have the right to a better life than they have here?"

Baxter grunted. "Sure they do, but we both know it's not realistic to believe every orphan or child will have a good life."

Addison closed his eyes. "I can't leave them here, Baxter. Not with the possibility they could get captured by any of the groups and forced to fight or live in a prison camp. I think we can do it. We only have another day or two in the DMZ, then we'll be able to cross over into UEA territory."

"Once that happens, we'll have to be extra careful not to get caught by the UEA soldiers. How do we keep little ones quiet during the night so a patrol doesn't find us? We need to think about those things before we take them on."

"I plan on stealing a truck once we get over the boundary. I think that'll help with the travel part of the journey. Until then, I know the little ones might not be able to keep up, but it's not like we can't carry them. They can't weigh any more than our packs do. We'll take turns." Addison glanced over at Baxter and saw the man smile.

"I knew that was going to be your decision the minute Dash mentioned there were little ones with him." Baxter brushed a kiss over Addison's lips. "You've a soft heart, my love."

Chapter Eleven

"Or a soft head," Addison muttered.

Baxter chuckled, so happy Addison had decided to take the children with them. He'd never doubted that was the decision his lover was going to come to, but sometimes it was hard to know what would be best for everyone.

He understood that traveling with little ones wasn't going to be easy, even with the help of Dash and Mariah. They would have to be extra careful to keep the children quiet, but Baxter was confident they would be able to do it.

After wrapping his arm around Addison's shoulders, Baxter pulled him closer. "We'll all help out, and you'll see taking them with us was the only choice you could've made."

Addison buried his face in the spot where Baxter's neck and shoulder met, and Baxter heard him breathe in. Keeping his mouth shut, he hoped Addison soaked up whatever kind of comfort he could get with Baxter embracing him.

He didn't know how long they sat there, quietly holding each other while they waited. Baxter wasn't sure if Addison had drifted off or not, but he didn't move just in case he had. There wasn't going to be a lot of down time once they crossed into UEA territory. Once into the enemy's space, they would need to move quickly to get to the Mexican border.

Addison's plan to steal a truck was a good one. Baxter made a mental note to give Franco and Markeo a heads-up on having the men keep an eye out for a vehicle to carry all of them. They couldn't risk stealing two, even though it might be better.

Baxter heard a throat being cleared, and he twisted slightly to look at the stall doorway. Markeo stood there, and Baxter nodded to let him know it was okay to speak.

"Dash and his group are here," Markeo said softly, but Baxter heard him just fine.

"We'll be right there. How do they look, Markeo?"

The corporal shrugged. "They're thin, but not too bad. I think they'll be able to keep up with a little help from us."

"Good."

Markeo left, and Baxter shifted enough to shake Addison. His lover jerked upright, narrowly missing clipping Baxter's chin with his head.

"Are they here?" Addison rubbed his hands into his eyes.

"Yes. Markeo says they don't look too bad and should be able to make it."

Addison shoved to his feet, then offered Baxter a hand up. "Let's go give them some reassurance, Baxter. We have a lot of ground to cover tomorrow and everyone needs to get some kind of rest."

"Yes, sir."

Baxter followed Addison back to the main part of the barn where all the men were gathered, except for Patterson and Alves, who were standing guard at the perimeter.

The children were huddled in the middle of the group, close to the fire. Synder was preparing meals for all of them while Dash talked quietly to the other GEs. The oldest girl had to be Mariah, and she eyed them all with fear flaring deep in her gaze.

Baxter didn't blame her. She was a pretty girl, just on the cusp of becoming a woman, and they were adult men who must look scary to her. When a girl didn't have the opportunity or ability to protect herself, the DMZ was a dangerous place. Baxter was sure Dash did his best to keep her and the others safe, but he wasn't much older or bigger than Mariah.

"I know you have no reason to believe this, miss, but we aren't going to hurt you or the little ones," he said to her.

She stiffened, then moved closer to Dash, and Baxter realized his all-black eye must have startled her. He stepped back to let Addison and the others deal with them. He didn't want to frighten them.

"I'm Addison."

Baxter watched as Addison introduced his men.

"You're coming with us to Mexico. Once we're in a safe place, you can decide whether you want to stay with us or make your own way in the world." Addison sighed. "The journey isn't going to be easy. It is going to be very hard. We'll do our best to keep you as protected as we can, but you must obey us, no matter what we say."

Glaring at him, Dash shook his head. "We'll listen to you within reason. If I think what you're saying is putting us into more danger, then I won't allow the others to do what you say."

Markeo pushed into the middle. "Boy, you need to think about what you're saying. We don't have to take you with us, and we're soldiers. We should know what's going to be dangerous for you and what won't be."

Baxter saw one of the little ones grab Mariah's hand while the other one pressed closer to Dash. He reached out to grip Markeo's arm, then jerked the man back.

"Let Addison talk, Corporal." Baxter glanced over at Dash. "The young man meant he wasn't going to let Mariah feel like she needed to lay down with one of us if we ordered her to."

"What?" All of the men shouted at once, while Dash and Mariah paled.

Addison shot them a quick look. "That will *never* happen, and if it does, you come tell me right away, Mariah, and I'll take care of it."

"What if it's you?" Mariah whispered.

Everyone chuckled as Addison took Baxter's hand to drag him back into the circle. Baxter tried to keep his gaze from meeting the little ones' eyes.

"Trust me. That will never happen, honey. I like men, not

136

women." Addison glanced at Dash. "And I mean men, not boys."

Dash didn't look convinced, but Baxter smiled.

"You'll just have to take us at our word, Dash, and keep a wary eye on us. You'll all learn to trust us as we travel together." Baxter squeezed Addison's hand. "If you still want to go with us?"

Mariah sighed. "We don't have any choice, sir. The little ones won't last much longer if we have to do this on our own. Do all of you prefer men?"

Baxter glanced around at the others. They all looked a little uncomfortable, and Baxter realized they weren't happy talking about sex with Mariah and the little ones there.

He started chuckling, drawing everyone's attention. "I think you're just going to have to accept the fact some of them might like women, Mariah, but they won't force you. If one of them does, he isn't the man I thought he was, and I'll deal with him."

Something in the tone of Baxter's voice must have convinced Mariah, or maybe it was the fact he looked scary with one totally black eye. Either way, she relaxed, which helped the little ones to calm down as well.

"Here are meals." Synder handed them out.

Baxter gestured to the bales closest to the fire. "Why don't you all sit there?"

Mariah and Dash herded the other two over, then they sat. Mariah helped them with their packets while Dash ate. When he finished, they switched, so Mariah could eat. The littlest one ate quickly, like he hadn't been fed in days.

"If you're not careful, you'll get sick," Baxter warned him gently.

The boy stared at Baxter for a second, then swallowed. He looked a little worried, but he slid off his bale to make his way over to Baxter. Not sure what to do, Baxter crouched so he was closer to the child's height.

"What happened to your eye?" He pointed at Baxter's

eye.

"I had something implanted that didn't agree with my head. When they took it out, my eye turned black like this." He tapped the side of his head.

"Did it hurt?"

Baxter didn't move as the little boy touched his cheek right under Baxter's eye. He wasn't going to lie to the kid.

"Yeah, it did hurt pretty bad." Baxter shot Mariah a glance, but she didn't look worried. "What's your name, little one?"

He shrugged. "I don't know."

"What does he mean?" Baxter met Mariah's sad gaze.

"He's so young, he doesn't remember what his parents named him. We've just been calling him Little Bit." Mariah shrugged. "It's not ideal, but I guess we've just been waiting for him to pick a name for himself."

Baxter sat on the floor, and Little Bit climbed right into his lap without any more fear in his eyes. He carefully wrapped his arms around the boy, holding him close. It wasn't long before Little Bit was sound asleep, obviously feeling safe in Baxter's arms.

As Addison walked past him, Baxter felt him brush his hand over Baxter's hair. Holding a child while he slept was something Baxter never dreamed he'd experience, especially as a GE. They were never allowed anywhere near children because people worried the GEs would lose control and hurt them.

"Here. He likes to hold this while he's sleeping."

Baxter looked up to see Mariah standing next to him, holding out a ragged, dirty blanket. He took it, then tucked it into Little Bit's arms. He nodded toward the spot next to him, and Mariah sat. He leaned back against the barn wall and closed his eyes.

He didn't know how long he slept, but when Addison knelt in front of him, Baxter woke. Blinking to clear his vision, Baxter saw the soft gleam of love in Addison's gaze. His lover reached out to cup his cheek, then rubbed his thumb along Baxter's bottom lip.

"Why don't you take the kids into one of the stalls where they can sleep without us bothering them," Addison said softly.

Baxter frowned at the weight on his shoulder, and he glanced over to see Mariah had fallen asleep as well. She rested against him, and it seemed she trusted him enough to let down her guard.

"Okay. Can you get Dash and the other little one?" Baxter reached over to tap Mariah on the knee. "Mariah, wake up for a second."

Addison nodded, then stood to walk over to where the other two were curled up on the floor. Mariah woke up in a hurry, glancing around in a panic until she spied Dash and the little ones.

"Addison said we should have you four sleep in one of the front stalls. The men will be coming and going because of guard duty, and he wants the little ones to rest well," Baxter told her.

She nodded. "That's a good idea, and maybe Dash can get some sleep. He tries so hard to take care of us, but he's still young, too, and shouldn't have so much responsibility."

Baxter agreed. "Well, you're with us now, and we'll do our best to keep all of you safe."

"I don't think you're going to get Dash to let you take care of him," Mariah said.

"Probably not, but we'll keep an eye on him while we teach him to take care of himself. No man—no matter his age—wants to feel like he needs help." Baxter understood how Dash felt.

Mariah pushed to her feet, then took Little Bit from him so he could stand. By the time they were ready to move, Dash and the younger girl had joined them. Baxter checked with Addison to see which stall the lieutenant wanted the kids in.

Addison pointed to the first one on the right. When they got in there, Baxter found a few blankets laid out already.

He left Dash and Mariah tucking the other two in and returned to Addison.

"Are they all right with their bed?" Addison touched Baxter on his hip when he joined him.

Baxter chuckled. "They would've been happy with just a dry, safe place to sleep. Getting clean blankets on top of that was more than they expected."

"True." Addison slid his arm around Baxter's waist, letting him rest against him. "We should probably get some sleep ourselves. The morning will get here soon enough, and I want to get closer to UEA territory before the day is over."

"Once we cross the border, do we continue moving by day?" Baxter asked as they made their way back to their stall.

Addison nodded. "Yes. Also, before we head out in the morning, we're going to strip all patches and remove anything that might give the enemy an instant sign we're AFF."

Baxter couldn't help the chuckle that escaped him. "Don't you think anyone just looking at us will know we're GEs? It's not like we blend in with normal people."

They really didn't look like normal Trues. Every one of the men in the unit, except for Addison, stood at least six-four and weighed in at around two hundred pounds of solid muscle. They all resembled each other in an unnatural way because the scientists used the same base DNA strand for all the GEs, except the officers. It was their way of insuring the GE units were perfectly matched in size and strength.

The differences between Baxter and Addison were both physical and mental. Addison's intelligence scores were higher than his. Addison was an officer, so he had to be smarter than Baxter and the rest of the men. Lieutenant was the highest position a GE could reach. Any rank above that was reserved for Trues, and it didn't matter whether the True was smarter or not.

Baxter lost track of his thoughts when Addison poked

him in the side. "What?"

"Stop standing there and lie down. There's not going to be a lot of rest once we get farther along in this journey." Addison knelt on the blanket.

After lying down, Baxter rolled over on his side, and Addison rested his arm over Baxter's waist, keeping him close. He breathed in Addison's familiar scent—a mixture of sweat, gun oil and male musk, but there was also a faint smell of sex mingled in. Baxter stuck out his tongue to take a quick lick of Addison's skin at the base of his throat.

"Baxter," Addison said, a slight warning in his tone, "we don't have time for that."

"I just wanted to taste you since you smell so good." Baxter rubbed his nose against Addison's jaw. "I know we can't do anything the rest of the night."

Addison chuckled. "I smell good? I stink of sweat, gun powder and cum. How is that good?"

"But you smell like both of us now, and I like that," Baxter admitted. "It makes me feel like I have a home now. As long as I can smell myself on you, and you on me, it's like I'll never be alone."

He ducked his head to press his face into Addison's shirt. He hadn't meant to say that particular thought aloud. Addison didn't need to know how desperately Baxter depended on him. Hell, he outweighed Addison by thirty pounds and was taller than him by three inches. Someone would think Baxter should be the one taking care of Addison instead of the other way around.

Addison pulled him closer, twining their legs and arms until it would be almost impossible for anyone to tell where one of them began and the other ended.

Baxter felt Addison brush his ear with his lips before he said, "You're never going to be alone as long as I'm breathing, Baxter. That's a promise you can count on me keeping forever."

"I love you," he whispered.

"I love you, too, Baxter. I always have, and once we get

to Mexico, we won't have to worry about fighting or dying. All we'll need to think about is loving."

When Addison finished speaking, he crushed Baxter to his chest, and Baxter relaxed. If Addison said it would happen, then it would. Addison never accepted defeat, no matter how difficult or dangerous a mission became. If anyone could get their ragtag band of people through enemy territory to safety, it would be Addison.

Baxter pressed his lips to Addison's chest, then got his hands between them so he could start unbuttoning Addison's shirt. While he worked, he waited for Addison to stop him, but his lover simply reached down to fumble with the fastenings of Baxter's pants.

Abandoning Addison's shirt, Baxter mimicked what Addison was doing. He wanted to feel his skin against Addison's. When their cocks were freed from their confining pants, both men groaned. Then Baxter wrapped his hand around their erections, and Addison grunted as Baxter started pumping up and down.

His callused hand was rough against the velvet-smooth skin of their cocks, and the friction caused a little bit of pain and pleasure. Baxter rested his forehead against Addison's, panting while he jacked them off.

"Oh, Baxter," Addison moaned, his hips moving in time with Baxter's strokes. "Tighter. Faster."

There wasn't a lot of room for Baxter to maneuver, so he couldn't really go much faster than he was, but he could tighten his grip. Suddenly, Addison entwined his fingers with Baxter's, and Baxter slammed his mouth against Addison's to muffle their strangled cries.

Baxter started moving his hips as well and too soon his climax tore through him. He spurted cum all over their fingers, then a few seconds later, Addison did the same. Their combined seed eased the roughness slightly, giving them time to work their cocks until there was nothing left for either of them to give.

After unwrapping his hand, Baxter rolled over on his back,

gasping for air. Addison stayed close to him, but somehow managed to get something for him to wipe his hand on. He cleaned up, then handed the piece of cloth back to Addison before snuggling close to his lover again.

"Rest now," Addison whispered against Baxter's temple. "Tomorrow is the beginning, and we're going to need all our strength to get everyone to Mexico without problems."

Baxter nodded. "There'll be problems. We're AWOL and considered prime enemies of the UEA. We can hope that when we get into UEA territory, they're the only ones we have to deal with. Getting over the border is going to be the most dangerous thing we've done to date."

"I know, but I have to look positive in front of all of them, love. If I look worried, they'll worry." Addison sounded tired.

"They'll worry anyway, but stay strong in front of them, then at night you can lean on me. Tell me all your concerns, and we'll do what we can to work them out." Baxter nuzzled Addison's jaw. "I love you, Addison, and I'm going to be with you through everything.

"And I'll be there with you," Addison promised before he sighed. "We should get our clothes back in order. Never know when we'll have to roll out of bed, and none of the other guys want to see our junk."

He laughed as he reached down to button his pants back up. "You're right. Do you think they'll find people to love when we get to safety?"

Addison shrugged. "I don't even know if they'll stick around once we're safe, Baxter. The guys might decide to go their own ways. We've been together since our unit was formed. And all we've known was fighting and training."

Baxter looked forward to the days when he didn't have to be on guard or carry a gun with him everywhere he went.

Oh, he understood Mexico wasn't going to be the paradise they wanted it to be. They would have problems finding jobs and places to live, but as long as they worked together, they'd probably end up being happier than if they'd stayed

143

in the AFF.

Well, they'd be alive at least, and the way True politics was going, odds were good they wouldn't have survived much longer. The scientists were cranking out more and more GEs because their True leaders were using them as pure cannon fodder, and they were dying at a far more rapid rate than the scientists originally had planned.

Once their clothes were back in order, they wrapped their arms around each other, entwining legs and arms. Addison rested his head on Baxter's chest, and Baxter laid his cheek on top of Addison's head.

"Do you think the supreme commander would ever do something to help GEs? Maybe once the war is over with?" Baxter had started thinking about Cameron and his brother earlier while they'd been taking care of the children.

"I have no idea. Just because his lover is a GE doesn't mean the supreme commander really cares about the rest of us. Plus I have no idea how long this war will continue. Maybe by the time it's over with, he won't be in power anymore, especially if the Trues find out he's been sleeping with a GE."

"Right, but if they haven't found out yet, don't you think he might be able to get away with it?" He pursed his lips, then said, "Do you think Cameron made it out okay?"

The thought of the doctor being caught and punished for helping them get away bothered Baxter. It wasn't like they had been friends or anything like that, but Cameron had taken a huge risk to get the camera out of Baxter's eye. That was something he couldn't overlook. He wished he could've convinced the doctor to come with them.

"I'm sure he's fine, Baxter." Addison tightened his embrace. "We can't save everyone. We have to choose our battles, and those four kids in the other stall is the battle we're going to take on."

"You're right, but I hope we find out he's okay at some time in the future," he muttered, not caring if that made him sound sappy or not.

"So do I, love. So do I."

Closing his eyes, Baxter relaxed enough to drift off, knowing there were others to watch out for danger.

* * * *

A few minutes or an hour later—Baxter wasn't sure how long it had been—he woke suddenly, staring out into the shadows. What had awakened him? Blinking, he tried to get his eyes to focus, and while his right eye was still blank, he swore he saw a small, dark shadow by the opening of the stall.

Untangling himself from Addison, Baxter rose to his knees, then moved a little closer to the shade. As he got closer, the image blurred, then cleared to show him Little Bit standing there.

"What are you doing up, Little Bit? You should be sleeping."

He held out his hand, and Little Bit dashed over to him, throwing his tiny body into Baxter's arms. Little lips pressed to his ear, Little Bit whispered, "I couldn't sleep. Got scared."

"That's all right. Why don't you come lie down with Lieutenant Addison and me? We'll keep the monsters away."

Shifting slowly so as to not wake Addison, Baxter lay back before wiggling into Addison's body again. Little Bit snuggled closer, and within seconds, the boy was sound asleep, his hand clasped tightly around Baxter's. He grasped his blanket in the other.

"Did he have nightmares?" Addison put his mouth near Baxter's ear, obviously not wanting to wake up Little Bit.

"That's what he said. It has to be upsetting, getting told he's traveling with a group of large men after having seen men hurt each other and him, too, for all we know." Baxter let his head drop back to Addison's shoulder. "We have to keep them safe, Addison."

145

"We will, and they'll be able to make their own lives when we're safe."

"What if I don't want them to go away once we've got a home?" Baxter ducked his head.

"They have to decide for themselves what they want, Baxter, but we'll offer our home to them. That's what we're doing by running away. We're finding a place to call our own."

Baxter nodded as he pulled the child closer. The future wouldn't be easy, but he believed there would be a happy ending when they were done.

Chapter Twelve

Addison gathered his small group in front of the barn as the sun peeked over the horizon. He studied all of his men, armed to the teeth with weapons to get them through the DMZ and UEA territory. Dash and Mariah each piggybacked a little one.

He shot Baxter a concerned glance, and his lover grinned before winking. Baxter's right eye was still black, so Addison was going to operate on the assumption his sight was never going to return. He knew Baxter would adjust, like he had with his head injury.

Adjusting and adapting made GEs what they were. GEs never stopped evolving, and Addison had a feeling the next generation would be looking for something more than serving the Trues. He wished them well if they chose to rise up, but he and his family would be out of the country by then.

"All right, everyone, listen up. Now we have the four younger ones, we have to be a little more diligent in scoping things out." Addison nodded toward Dash and Mariah. "I know you two will do your best to keep an eye on the littler ones, and they know to keep quiet as best they can."

Dash nodded, and the youngest children nodded as well, bringing a smile to Addison's face. He ruffled Little Bit's hair then looked at the men.

"We'll surround them. Keep them in the middle of the group. Markeo, I want you and Alves in the lead, one to each side of the trail. Franco, Synder, Gephardt and Patterson, two of you on the left and right of the kids. Spaced out accordingly. Baxter and I will bring up the rear."

Everyone spread out, taking their places, and Addison found himself happy for a moment that he was on this journey with this group of men. Each one would lay down his life for the others. That kind of loyalty couldn't be taught. It was earned with respect and the knowledge that each man in the team would have the others' backs if necessary.

Maybe the gene to develop those traits had been interwoven into the GEs' DNA, because Addison had only seen that level of loyalty among the units of his own kind. Oh, there probably were True units and squads that cared deeply about one another and who would give up their lives to keep their comrades safe, but Addison hadn't run into any of those. They were probably kept close to the supreme commander to protect him, instead of wasted on frontline battles that never seemed to end.

"Addison?"

Glancing up, he saw Baxter staring at him. "What?"

"We're ready. We should get moving, so we're close enough to the border between the DMZ and the UEA by nightfall. It was your plan to cross over during the darkness, right?" Baxter held his gun loosely in his hands — his lover had been one of the best shots in the unit. Only time would tell whether Baxter would get that back with only one eye to see from.

"Yes, that was my plan. I might have to adjust when we get there. Depends on how well the kids are doing." He motioned toward their four new companions.

"If it comes to that, we can carry the little ones to give Mariah and Dash a break. They aren't as heavy as our packs," Baxter pointed out. "It won't be that hard to carry them. Whoever carries a kid, his pack gets carried by one of the other men."

"True." He looked back at the barn, sweeping it and the ground around it with his gaze, seeing if they'd left any sign they were there. "All right, gentlemen, let's move out."

They headed down the faint trail Alves had discovered

148

that led in the direction of UEA territory. Addison kept his eyes moving, watching for any kind of movement on his side of the trail. He didn't worry about any of the rest because he knew they'd do their jobs.

Addison also kept an eye on the kids, making sure they took breaks often. Moving slower than the unit usually did wasn't a bad thing. They were more likely to spot any rebel patrols or UEA spies that way.

Around noon, they took a break for a quick meal in the hidden clearing Markeo had found for them. Addison saw the way Markeo watched Dash and wondered if there might be something there, though he also knew Markeo would keep his hands to himself because no one had any real idea how old Dash was.

Then he took matters into his own hands. "Dash, how old did you say you are?"

Dash frowned, then said, "I'm at least eighteen, sir. That's why I'm trying to make sure anyone doesn't catch me. I don't want to fight in someone else's war."

Addison saw a flash of relief cross Markeo's face and smiled. Well, there was one worry gone. Then something Dash said caught his attention.

"Someone else's war? You're not from around here?"

Dash shook his head. "Nope. My parents were from the Northern Territories. They came down here to find work, then the UEA invaded and we were stuck. They were taken by the AFF to one of their training camps. My mom had hidden me away, so the soldiers didn't find me."

"I guess it worked out in the end, right? Though I am sorry about your parents." Addison checked his watch, then motioned to them to clean up. "We need to head out now."

Dash smiled in acknowledgment of Addison's words, but didn't say anything else as they headed out to get to the edge of the border before nightfall.

As dark eased over them like a warm, familiar blanket, Alves found them shelter in a bombed out house just a few feet from the border. Addison had the men strip and clean their weapons.

"Mariah, see if you can convince the kids to sleep for a bit. I don't want to move out until closer to shift change. There should be a gap as they change over. I want to exploit that."

"Yes, sir."

He stepped out of the house, staying in the shadows as he studied the clearly marked line in the dirt. On the other side of that line was the true beginning of their run for freedom.

A soft laugh drifted to him from where the others were setting up a temporary camp. Addison turned to look at them and spotted Baxter staring at him.

Baxter mouthed, "I love you," and Addison said it back because, really, what it all came down to was having the people he loved safe and sound in a place that wouldn't use them as cannon fodder in a war that would never be won.

He walked back to where Baxter stood, then encircled the man's waist. It wasn't very comfortable, but he didn't care. All he wanted to do was hold Baxter for a little while before the shit hit the fan. Addison wasn't naïve enough to believe they would make it to Mexico unscathed.

Looking at the people who were with him, he hoped they would all make it, but he was too realistic to think that would happen. Yet he was going to do his damnedest to ensure the children got through just fine.

Baxter relaxed against him, though he knew his lover was staying alert to the world around them. "We'll get through this just fine, Addison. Our unit is the best out there, and I think the doctor might help us a little in this."

"I very much doubt the supreme commander is going to help an entire unit of his GEs go AWOL," Addison said with a soft chuckle.

"You never know. We didn't know he'd have a GE as a lover, so maybe he could be swayed to our side." Baxter shrugged. "It's not like we're going over to the other side. Hell, we're heading to a neutral country where we won't be fighting anyone."

As the night progressed, Addison and Baxter took their turns at patrolling around the shelter. The children napped until Addison decided they'd waited long enough. Mariah fed them, while Dash talked softly with Markeo.

Baxter nudged him and nodded in their direction. Addison smiled, but didn't say anything. He got all of them up and moving within minutes. He'd studied and memorized as many maps as he could get his hands on.

"All right, everyone. About twenty klicks from here is a small farm. They'll have a vehicle we can borrow. My plan never had us walking from here to Mexico, so this won't change things." Addison handed Franco a GPS. "We'll follow these coordinates to the target. I mapped out the safest possible route, but we all know how things can go to hell without any warning."

The men and Dash nodded. Mariah grimaced, but she seemed to understand what Addison was saying.

"Okay, Franco and Gephardt, you take point. The rest of you spread out around Dash, Mariah and the children. Baxter and I will take up the rear again."

"Yes, sir."

His group set out, and Addison had to admit Dash and Mariah moved as quietly as his men. Maybe their ability came from living in the DMZ, avoiding both sides of the war. They wouldn't have survived for as long as they had if they couldn't take care of themselves.

Several times during their journey, Franco would signal everyone to freeze, and they would all crouch. The GEs would have their guns ready, while Dash and Mariah would be ready to run with the children. Addison appreciated how vigilant everyone was, but his gut said they would reach the farm safely.

Once they reached the outskirts of the farm, Addison called a halt. He brought all his people together to give more instructions.

"Alves, I want you and Patterson to stay here with the children. The rest of us will recon the house and barn. My gut tells me there's no one around, but we have to make sure." Addison slid off his pack and gestured for the others to do so also.

"You know what to do if we're captured or don't come back," he told Alves.

"Yes, sir, but we'll see you back here in forty minutes." Alves saluted him.

Addison nodded. "Set your watches, gentlemen. Someone will back here to get you in forty."

He led the way from the edge of the woods across the fields toward the two buildings. Using hand signals, he split the unit into two squads of three. Markeo, Gephardt and Synder headed toward the barn, while Addison, Baxter and Franco went in the direction of the house.

They circled it, using all their senses and the equipment they'd managed to bring with them to check to make sure the house was empty. After finding no signs of occupation, Addison made entrance into the building and they swept through the place to clear it. When they rendezvoused in the kitchen, the other three were there.

"Place is clear," Baxter told him.

"The barn is clear as well. Doesn't look like there's been any animals in there for a while." Markeo glanced over to his right. "But someone must've been living here in the last couple of days. The electricity is on and the refrigerator is running."

"That's good. Synder, check to see if there are any provisions here. We can't turn a light on in case someone goes by and sees it, but we can have warm food at least." Addison barked out the orders, making sure all the men knew what they needed to do before he went back to gather the others.

"Do you want me to go with you?" Baxter asked as Addison got ready.

Addison studied Baxter and saw the small lines of pain bracketing his lover's mouth. "No. I can get there on my own, and I'll have the others with me on the way back."

Baxter nodded, and Addison could tell he wasn't feeling good.

"Why don't you take some painkillers and lie down for a little while? The rest of us can take turns on watch tonight."

"I can do my part, Addison," Baxter protested, but his shoulders drooped like he was losing his battle with the pain he was in.

He stepped up to cup Baxter's cheek, then rested his forehead against Baxter's. "We all know you can do your part, love, but you're in pain and when you're injured, you need to rest to recover. We've all been there, and we'll probably all be there again before this journey is over."

"I just don't want to slow any of you down, and I don't want the men think you're giving me special treatment because of your feelings for me."

Addison chuckled, then pressed a kiss to Baxter's lips before stepping back. "As much as I do love you, I'm not treating you any different than I would anyone else. We have shelter again tonight, so everyone is going to get some sleep. It's going to get harder from here on in to find shelter without having to deal with other people."

Baxter sighed as he nodded. "You're right. I'll make sure food is ready, then I'll head up to get some sleep. I hate this," he confessed.

"I know, Baxter, but the pain will go away as your body adjusts to the change. Now go on and lie down. Let Gephardt worry about the food." He kissed Baxter again, then left.

He had no problem finding his way across the fields to where they'd left the others. He was twenty feet out from the rendezvous spot when Patterson confronted him. After confirming his identity, they rounded up the children and Alves to return to the house.

* * * *

A few hours later, the children had all settled into their

153

beds, and the men were down in the kitchen. Baxter had joined them after a while, and when Addison told his friends to sit, Baxter sat next to him.

"All right, I'm going to let you all in on my plans. I've been over our escape routes for months now, ever since I found out we were being sent to Alpha Two. There wasn't any way I wasn't going to take the chance to get the hell out of AFF territory when we were this close to freedom." Addison stood, then started to pace.

"But we really aren't that close to freedom, sir. We still have a helluva lot of UEA territory between us and Mexico," Franco pointed out.

"True, but we're closer now than we were yesterday. We need to keep that outlook or we're going to get discouraged." Addison clasped his hands behind his back.

Baxter laughed. "We're GEs, Addison. We don't get discouraged. That emotion—or genetic disposition— wasn't bred into us. That's one of the reasons why we're sent on suicide missions. We don't give up, and we have to die before we fail."

Addison cringed because he knew Baxter was telling the truth. The Trues had created GEs to insure they would never retreat from a fight. GEs didn't recognize fear. They didn't tire as easily as Trues. They often were the last ones standing during long battles because they simply didn't understand how to quit fighting.

So many of his fellow GEs were dead, thrown into the meat grinder of this stupid war, and Addison had killed more than his share of UEA soldiers, men fighting for their country. And as much as he'd like to say he was fighting for his, Addison acknowledged he and his fellow GEs didn't have any home. No one would accept them.

What he truly feared, deep in his heart, was that when the war was over, no matter who won, the GEs would be rounded up like cattle and slaughtered. The humans would destroy them or put them into camps, to use them for manual labor or anything else the Trues wanted the GEs to do. Until there were none left to threaten the Trues.

Yes, GEs weren't created to fear anything, yet Addison was afraid and, as he studied the faces of the men he'd fought and killed with, he knew he would do everything in his power to make sure they survived. He wanted them to live in a country—and a world—that didn't see them as monsters.

"You're right, Baxter, but we need to tell the children that, so they don't get discouraged. This will be harder on them than it'll be on us. We're hardened soldiers, used to doing without and going days without sleep. They are Trues and fragile, no matter what Dash would like us to think." Addison smiled.

Markeo grunted, then said, "I'll keep an eye on them, sir. But I think we should take turns carrying them, so Dash and Mariah don't wear themselves out."

"Good idea. Now I want us to sit and plan out the rest of our journey. I've memorized maps and put in the coordinates of different places we should be able to find shelter in, but we'll be doing a lot of traveling by night and on the road. We'll take one of the vehicles left here as far as we can, until we're either stopped or we run out of gas."

The men started murmuring among themselves as he pulled hand-drawn maps out of his pack. They discussed the logistics of moving eight large men, two teenagers and two little children across enemy lines without being detected.

None of them believed they'd be able to just waltz over the border into Mexico. There was a fierce battle coming, but they'd trained for those all their lives.

For the first time, they'd be fighting for a better future for themselves. They would be fighting for their own lives and homes, instead of the lives and homes of Trues who would never acknowledge their existence. They had a reason to fight instead of following orders. Addison had a feeling that would be far more effective than anything Tilton or any of their commanding officers could've have said to them.

155

After three hours of solid planning, he sent Synder and Franco out to guard the perimeter and told the others to grab some shut-eye. The watches would be for four-hour shifts. They would stay at the house for one more day and night, then leave at sunrise the third day.

"I'm going to rest." Addison stood and poked Baxter in the shoulder. "Why don't you come with me?"

Baxter headed out of the kitchen as Addison looked over at Markeo, who just winked at him while making a shooing motion. Thank God his men were open-minded enough to accept what was going on between Baxter and him. Of course, Addison admitted to himself, ultimately it didn't matter what they thought. He would love Baxter in the face of any opposition.

He stared at Baxter's back as they climbed the stairs to the second floor, where they took the room at the front of the house. The children were in the back, closer to the stairs and easier escape in case someone attacked the house. As far as he and his men were concerned, the children were more important than their lives. Their mission had changed from freedom for themselves to keeping the children safe.

He stripped off his gear, piling it close to the door, but kept his rifle with him. Baxter did the same, putting their equipment together. Addison tackled him onto the bed and smiled as Baxter's surprised laughter burst out.

They wrestled until Addison had Baxter pinned to the mattress. He settled between the man's legs, then rocked his groin into Baxter's.

"Oh God." Baxter groaned, pushing back against Addison. "Can we fuck, sir?"

Addison nuzzled along Baxter's jaw, then nipped his chin. "What did I tell you about calling me sir?"

"Sorry." He didn't sound sorry.

"Yes, we're going to fuck. I'm going to pound your ass because I want you so badly, my love." He dove in to take Baxter's mouth with determination.

While dueling with Baxter for control over the kiss,

Addison started fumbling with the Velcro that kept his clothes on. He growled low, frustrated at not being able to get Baxter naked as fast as he wanted.

He grunted when Baxter flexed, and he wound up on the bottom with Baxter straddling his hips. Before he could do anything about it, Baxter tore his shirt off and tossed it over his shoulder. Addison lifted his hands to run his fingers over Baxter's muscular chest, but Baxter rolled off the bed to start taking off his pants.

"You need to get naked, Addison. If we're going to fuck, I need you without clothes."

"Fuck. You're right." Addison jumped to his feet and stripped, stumbling around when his pants caught up on his boots. "Shit!"

Baxter chuckled while dropping to his knees. "Sit. I'll get these off for you."

He dropped to the edge of the bed, trailing his hands over Baxter's broad shoulders and caressing the outside shells of the man's ears. Baxter shook his head, and Addison smiled. He slid his hands down to rub his thumbs over Baxter's flat, copper-colored nipples. Loving how they hardened beneath his touch, Addison pinched them, then added a little twist.

Hissing, Baxter yanked off Addison's boots, then threw them out of the way. Addison spread his thighs as Baxter pushed into his personal space before dipping his head to suck Addison's cock.

"Holy fuck," he swore, as the head of his shaft hit the back of Baxter's throat.

Baxter didn't stop when Addison gripped his head and started thrusting into his mouth. Addison figured his lover would stop him if he got too rough, but he couldn't help moving. The feel of Baxter's tongue on his cock was something Addison would never forget, and something he wanted to feel again and again.

He moaned as Baxter fondled his balls, then tugged roughly. "Oh shit, Baxter."

157

Addison wouldn't let him move to bob his head, and while Baxter played with his balls, he didn't struggle in Addison's hold. As the tingling at the base of his spine built, Addison inhaled sharply.

"Back off, Baxter. I want to come in your ass, not your mouth." One more hard suck, and Addison gently shoved Baxter away. "Crawl up on the bed, love."

He couldn't help but laugh at how fast Baxter moved to get on the bed before lying on his back. After scrambling back to the bed, he lifted one of Baxter's legs to rest the man's ankle on his shoulder. He coated his fingers with spit. Circling Baxter's puckered hole, he pressed just the tip inside.

Baxter bore down, taking more in as Addison wrapped his other hand around Baxter's cock. He stroked it, then breached Baxter's ass with two fingers. Soon Baxter was rocking between his hand and fingers, and Addison watched as sweat began to bead on Baxter's skin.

"Soon, Addison," Baxter warned, so Addison backed off.

Addison spit into his palm, then coated his own erection. Lifting both of Baxter's legs over his arms, Addison positioned himself at Baxter's hole, then slowly pushed in.

Addison was gentle until the flared head of his shaft popped through the ring of muscle, then he shoved as far into Baxter as he could. Baxter bit his lip, and it was obvious he didn't want to make any more noise. Maybe he didn't want to risk waking the kids up. All he wanted was to make Baxter come and ride the man through his climax.

Baxter braced his hands against the headboard, moving in counterpoint to Addison. They fell into a perfect rhythm, and soon Addison could feel his climax racing through his body until he cried out as he came, flooding Baxter's ass with his cum.

He managed to pry one of his hands from Baxter's waist to wrap it around his lover's cock. A few hard tugs, and Baxter's semen coated Addison's hand. They continued to move, slowing as their bodies stopped trembling and jerking.

Addison let Baxter's legs go, then collapsed at his side. Baxter winced as Addison slid from him, but rolled over to embrace Addison. They needed to clean up before they slept, yet Addison wasn't completely sure he'd be able to move any time soon.

Only a few minutes passed before his heart rate was back under his control and he could breathe without panting. He climbed out of bed, then shuffled to his canteen. Picking up his T-shirt, he soaked it before cleaning off himself and Baxter.

He tossed the shirt to the floor, then gathered up the rest of their clothes. "We should get dressed. Just in case we have to make a hasty exit."

Baxter nodded, but didn't say anything. Addison pulled out a dry T-shirt. After dressing, they lay back down, arms and legs entwined. He rested his cheek on the top of Baxter's head. Addison ran his hand up and down Baxter's back, hoping to soothe the man into sleep.

"You should rest, Baxter," Addison suggested.

"I know, but sometimes I'm afraid if I close my eyes, when I open them again, I won't be able to see out of either eye," Baxter confessed.

Addison pulled him closer. "If that happens, then we'll figure out a way to help you."

Baxter huffed. "I'd be a hindrance. I'd slow you all down. You'd have to leave me behind."

"No one gets left behind, especially you. I love you with every atom in me, Baxter, and the one thing I will never do is abandon you because you can't see, or are injured in any way." Addison closed his eyes, breathing in the familiar scent of Baxter's sweat. "Do you ever think we might have been made for each other?"

Baxter's chuckle warmed Addison's heart. "Addison, my love, we were created in a lab by men who planned to use us to fight their war. I doubt love was on their minds."

His lover was right, but Addison had a feeling that maybe

something else—or someone else—had had a hand in creating a man like Baxter, who was the perfect person for Addison.

"Maybe you're right," he conceded. "We should rest, and I'll be here when you wake up, Baxter, and you'll be able to see. Nothing is going to happen to you as long as I'm here to prevent it."

Baxter sighed, and Addison whispered a kiss over the man's temple. He stayed silent, just trailing his fingers over Baxter's back and arm. Soon the steady tempo of Baxter's breathing alerted Addison to the fact Baxter had fallen asleep.

Addison closed his eyes, letting go of his vigilance for a little while. The other men in his unit could protect them for a few hours.

Chapter Thirteen

Baxter made his way into the kitchen, where he found the others getting ready to eat breakfast. Addison gestured toward a plate of eggs, bacon and toast sitting on the table.

"Eat up. We need to take advantage of the extra calories while they're available. Markeo and Alves went to the barn to see if the truck works. If it does, we'll take it until it runs out of gas. Then we'll see if we can't find another one."

"We're going to steal vehicles to make our way through UEA territory to the border?" Dash asked from where he sat next to Rebecca, one of the children.

Little Bit came over to sit next to Baxter. When Baxter had finished and pushed his chair away from the table, Bit climbed into his lap. He wrapped his arms around the boy, taking care not to hold him too tightly.

"I think that's the only way we're going to get across this land without getting spotted sooner rather than later." Addison rubbed the back of his neck. "I'm not arrogant enough to believe my plan is foolproof. At some point, they'll discover us, and we'll have to fight, but I'm hoping we'll be close enough to the border to make a run for it."

Dash nodded. "I guess it makes as much sense as anything else."

"If you have a better plan, I'd be happy to hear it." Addison stared at the boy.

"Nah. I never really planned how to escape this place. Only how to survive it." Dash checked to make sure the other children had eaten and Mariah helped clean them up.

The rumble of a vehicle caught their attention, and Patterson went to the front of the house, while Synder checked out of the back door.

"It's Corporal Markeo, sir. I guess he got the truck running," the private informed them.

"Good. Okay, everyone, round up all your stuff and some blankets." Addison dropped some coins on the counter while Baxter helped the kids pack up.

Once everyone was ready, they raced from the house and got inside the large bed of the truck with as little fuss as possible. Addison sat up front with Markeo and Alves. Baxter stayed under cover in the back, making sure their band of travelers was as comfortable as they could make them.

Gephardt and Franco took up positions at the rear of the vehicle, their rifles at the ready, in case of trouble. They stopped at the front of the house to pick up Patterson, then they headed out.

The driveway leading out to the road was rough, and Baxter gritted his teeth each time his ass hit the bed of the truck. *Shit.* Maybe letting Addison fuck him the night before a mission like this wasn't the best idea. He was going to be very sore by the time they stopped for the night.

"What should we do?" Mariah glanced around at the men. "What did you do while you were heading out on missions?"

Synder shrugged. "We talked about the mission. What our jobs were going to be. What the objective was."

Baxter didn't think that was appropriate conversation for children, even older ones like Dash and Mariah. He pursed his lips, thought for a moment, then said, "What do you think Mexico will be like?"

Patterson shot him a half smile, like he knew what Baxter was doing. "I think it's going to be warm."

"Maybe not as cold as it gets around here," Dash said. "I'd like that."

"I like snow. You can make snowmen with it," Little Bit spoke up, and Baxter smiled.

"You're right, but, hey, in Mexico, you can make

162

sandcastles. We'll find a place close to the ocean, and you can all play on the beach all day." Baxter rested back against the cab of the truck, keeping his rifle close but relaxing slightly.

Any danger they might encounter would be seen way before they made contact, and he trusted the men around him to keep their eyes open while he tried to distract the kids. Mariah and Dash helped him as he wove a tale about what living in Mexico would be like.

Of course, he had no real idea what Mexico was going to be like. It had become a dream destination for the people caught in the war. When the UEA had invaded, Mexico had closed its borders, and the drug cartels had armed the populace to keep the war from spilling over into their country.

And while the Mexicans should've been less than thrilled that the cartels had taken over their home, they weren't. The cartels had divided the country into parts and ruled them far more democratically than the AFF and the UEA did their nations.

As far as Baxter was concerned, the most difficult part of the whole mission would be getting across the border. The Mexicans guarded their country fiercely against people jumping the border, which was ironic, considering how jealously America had done the same thing decades ago before the war.

After a while, the children fell asleep and the men chatted quietly among themselves. Baxter closed his eyes, breathing slowly to ease the pressure in his head. Having a blind spot in his sight was difficult, but he could tell his brain was already adjusting to the loss. The sight in his other eye was getting sharper, and his hearing was better than it had been before the camera had been removed.

Even the pain was lessening, though it was still there. It wasn't so bad that he couldn't think. He should've known Addison would know what he was talking about when he'd told Baxter he'd adapt. A GE's body was built to adjust to any condition and circumstance. He could withstand colder or hotter temperatures than a True, go longer without sleep and hike farther than they could. It was what he'd been created for, and those genetic mutations were going to help him survive.

A knock on the window had him looking behind him to meet Addison's gaze through the glass. He slid the small window open.

"Yes, sir."

"We have a truck headed our way. I doubt we'll get stopped, but if we do, just try to stay quiet. We're fine as long as no one looks in the back." Addison gestured toward the front of the vehicle.

Baxter took a quick look to see the outline of another truck headed their way. He nodded at Addison, then shut the window before pulling a tarp over the truck bed to block anyone's view.

"Did you hear that?"

The other men nodded as they settled in surrounding the children. They would take the brunt of an attack if someone came to search the back. It might give the kids a chance to get away before they could be taken captive.

The rumble of the approaching truck got louder as it drove closer, then they all instinctively ducked as it passed, even though the driver wouldn't have been able to see them. Gephardt had let the tarp down at the back as well, so no one would be able to look in.

The rest of the ride during the day was just as tension-filled, but Baxter did his best to keep the young ones calm and entertained. They passed several other vehicles on the road and, thankfully, none of them were military or interested in stopping them.

Addison told them that he'd found a spot on a map where they could spend the night. It wasn't the best shelter, but it would work, and they still had enough gas left to go all day tomorrow.

They parked the truck just inside the tree line, so if a plane came overhead, they would be hidden. Starting a fire under the trees ensured no one would see the smoke, either.

Working quickly, they got a meal cooked for the kids, and after they'd eaten, Synder put the fire out while Dash helped the children settle down in the back of the truck. The adults gathered outside to decide who would take which watch and who would pair up with whom.

Baxter offered to take the third watch, the darkest part of the night, but he'd always enjoyed that time. Usually there wasn't anyone else awake with him, so he could try to organize his thoughts and emotions.

"I'll stand with you," Dash offered before Addison could say anything.

"Are you sure? You'll be able to get some sleep once we're back on the road, but if your body isn't used to it, it'll be hard to stay awake." Baxter wasn't going to turn Dash's offer down. He knew the younger man wanted to pull his own weight.

"I've done this before. Mariah and I would take turns keeping watch. Two hours on. Two hours off." Dash shot Baxter a quick glance. "I know how not to get caught."

"True. Fine with me. Now go get some sleep. I'll wake you up when it's your turn." Baxter slapped Dash on the shoulder before motioning to the truck where the others slept.

"Thanks, sir." Dash disappeared under the tarp.

"What the fuck were you thinking?" Markeo pushed into Baxter's personal space.

Baxter was shocked at how upset the corporal was. "I'm thinking Dash wants to pull his weight, and if he feels he's up to keeping watch with us, then he should be able to."

"He could get himself killed." Markeo waved his hand wildly.

"Corporal, I'm thinking you don't really want to be doing that." Addison spoke up from where he stood, discussing strategy with Patterson.

He whirled to say something to Addison, and Baxter

165

grabbed his arm, dragging him farther away from the truck. He rested his hand on the back of Markeo's neck and held the man still.

Baxter leaned down to whisper in Markeo's ear, "I know you care for him, Markeo, but you need to get a hold of yourself. Dash is still young, and he feels like he has something to prove to you. To all of us actually."

"He's too young to do what we do, Bax. He shouldn't be put in that position," he protested.

Chuckling softly, Baxter said, "Dash has been taking care of himself, Mariah and the children for a long time now. I don't think he'll ever be young again in his soul. I wish he could be too young for all of this, but he wants to help and I'm not going to turn him down."

Markeo sighed, his shoulders drooping slightly. "I just don't want him hurt."

"None of us do, but we can't keep him back with the little ones and Mariah. He'll resent that, and you won't have any luck with him later on." Baxter squeezed Markeo's neck. "I'll keep an eye on him... You know that."

"I know, sir, and I'm sorry about getting in your face," Markeo apologized.

"It's all right, but you'd better not let Dash hear you trying to keep him from doing what he thinks is his job." Baxter nodded in the direction of the truck. "He believes he's responsible for those kids, and he was doing a damn good job before we showed up."

His friend nodded. "I know, but I've never felt like this about anyone before, and I'm freaking out a little. Besides, he's too young for me."

Baxter shrugged. "Maybe at the moment he is, but once we get to Mexico, you'll have time to get to know each other, and he can grow up a little."

Markeo didn't look convinced, but he gave Baxter a small smile. "Maybe, sir. I'll go take my post."

After patting the soldier on the back, Baxter joined Addison where he sat on the ground next to the truck. They leaned against the tire, sides pressed together. He rested his head on Addison's shoulder.

"First day down, Addison. That's good," Baxter said softly, not wanting to bother the kids or anyone else who might be sleeping.

"Yes, but I don't expect that to continue for long. We're going to have to fight at some point, Bax, and I'm worried about how the children will hold up." Addison laid his hand on Baxter's thigh.

Baxter covered Addison's hand with his. "I know, but I think they're all tougher than we think they are. They've made it this far together."

Addison hummed, but didn't say anything. Baxter lifted their entwined fingers to his mouth, then brushed a kiss over Addison's knuckles.

"We'll give our lives to get them to Mexico, and if the gods are willing, we won't lose anyone before we get across the border. I knew when we started this journey it wasn't going to be easy to achieve our freedom." Baxter pressed another kiss to his lover's hand. "But if anyone can get us through with the least amount of injuries, you can."

"You've always had so much confidence in me. More than I do myself, sometimes."

He encircled Addison's shoulders, bringing him closer to him. "You've never turned your back on me, Addison. I've always known you'd do anything for me. Plus I know you wouldn't have allowed us to run unless you had everything planned out beforehand."

Addison stayed silent, but Baxter knew his lover. The lieutenant wouldn't have chosen to run when he had if he hadn't thought his plan was as solid as he could make it. How had Addison gotten his hands on all the information and maps of UEA territory? Who had he talked to and convinced to help him gather all the intel?

Baxter wasn't going to ask Addison about it. The man had his secrets, and to keep them safe, Baxter knew he wouldn't share them unless absolutely necessary. He'd discovered how closely Addison held his knowledge, and learned it didn't pay to bother him about it. If and when Addison decided Baxter needed to know, he'd tell him.

"We're going to stay on this road for a couple of days, then I want us to head west for a few days before turning back south." Addison tightened his grip on Baxter's hand. "We need to reach the border in ten days' time."

"Will we be able to move fast enough with the kids to do that?" Baxter didn't want to know why they had a deadline.

Addison sighed. "As long as we keep traveling like we did today, we should be fine."

"All right. If you think we need to speed up, we can work something out," he informed his lover.

"I know, and you know I'll tell you if I think we need to move faster. I just don't want to wear everyone out before the tough part comes." Addison swallowed, then said, "And before we reach the border, I'm going to have to talk to all of you. There are some decisions that need to be made before we cross over into Mexico."

Baxter kissed Addison's cheek. "All right. Until then, we'll do our damnedest to get everyone safely to where we need to be."

"I've loved you for so many years, Baxter. I don't know what I'd have done if you'd died from your head wound." Addison wrapped his hand around Baxter's head to stroke his fingers over the scar there.

Baxter snuggled closer, loving how Addison made him feel safe, even though he was bigger than the lieutenant. There was just something about how Addison held him and how the man looked at him that told him that as long as this man drew breath, he would put himself between danger and Baxter.

"You wouldn't let me die, then you wouldn't them send me to one of the work compounds. If I hadn't already been in love with you, I would've fallen right then." He nuzzled along the edge of Addison's jaw. "We'll get through this, love, and spend the rest of our days on the beach in Mexico, playing with the kids and watching Markeo and Dash dance around each other."

Addison stiffened slightly for a second, then relaxed. "Yeah. I'd like that."

"Why don't you get some rest before you have to go on watch?"

"You should get some sleep as well." Addison slid down until he was lying on the ground, using his pack as a pillow.

Baxter didn't reply, just lay next to him. Addison brought him back against his chest and Baxter closed his eyes. He wasn't really tired, having caught a nap while riding in the truck, but having Addison pressed against him back-to-chest settled him. He let the sound of Addison's breathing ease him into sleep.

* * * *

Three days later, they found more gas for the truck, and they were happy about not having to abandon the vehicle. Addison never did say how he knew there would be gas at the deserted-looking station. Baxter chose not to ask. He was just glad they could still move fast.

None of the military or civilian vehicles they passed on the road seemed interested in checking them out, so again their luck was holding. Addison had them change directions, taking a side road that led them several hundred miles to the west.

The other men were curious about that move, but they—like Baxter—had learned not to question Addison. Their leader had good reasons for why he did things, and they trusted him.

As they turned back south, they found another stash of gas and food, and Baxter couldn't keep from saying something to Addison when they stopped for the night.

"We're getting really lucky with the gas situation. I thought we might have to abandon the truck a long time ago," he commented, as Addison crouched down next to

169

him by the fire.

Addison shot him a quick glance, then shrugged. "I might be using some secret supplies dumped by UEA soldiers."

"And how did you find out about them?" Baxter squinted at his lover. "It seems an odd thing for an AFF soldier to know."

"I might have come across some intel the Trues didn't want the GEs to know about, and also didn't want the UEA to know they knew." The lieutenant shifted before kneeling beside Baxter. "I'm doing my best to get us as close to the border as we can before we have to make a run for it. Those kids aren't going to be able to move fast. That means two of us will be compromised with carrying the youngest kids and not able to use our weapons. We'll be safe once we get into Mexico, but it's the getting there that'll be the problem."

Baxter set his MRE down, then stood. He held out his hand for Addison. "We need to take a walk."

Addison swallowed his food as he took Baxter's hand. "You're right. Someone else needs to know the whole plan in case something happens—"

Baxter pressed his fingers to Addison's mouth. "I'm not going to let you tempt fate by saying that. We've come too far for us to lose anyone."

Nodding, Addison pulled him down a small animal trail toward a stream they'd decided to camp by. Baxter leaned against one of the trees while Addison went to rinse his hands in the water.

"I wasn't going to ask. I was going to trust you and just do as you said." He rubbed his chin. "But I have to ask. How do you know we'll be safe once we get into Mexico?"

"I made a deal with José Gabriel Lopez."

Baxter felt his jaw drop at the mention of the head of the biggest Mexican cartel. The Lopez cartel controlled a majority of the Mexican west coast. José was the head of the council that ran all of the southern country. How had Addison managed to contact him?

"How the hell did that happen, and what the fuck made

170

you decide to make a deal with that particular devil?"

Addison sat on the bank, leaning back on his hands to stare up at the star-strewn night sky. "Shortly after your injury, I was approached by some members of the Lopez cartel. They'd managed to infiltrate the AFF. Hell, they've probably got men inside the UEA as well. Lopez believes in covering all his bases."

"And after being approached by this man, you didn't think to go to your commanding officer to expose him?" Baxter studied Addison. "That doesn't seem like you."

Snorting, Addison lifted one of his shoulders in a lopsided shrug. "Before you were hurt, sure. I'd have turned him in before he finished his pitch. But you were in the hospital, and no one could tell me whether you were going to live or not. If you did live, they couldn't say whether you'd be you again or not. I was having a hard time understanding why you had to die for a war we didn't even believe in."

Baxter clenched his hands, wanting to go to Addison, but needing to hear what his lover had to say first. He hadn't known him being wounded had shaken Addison to his very core. "But we're created to fight, whether we believe in the war or not. We aren't supposed to question orders."

Baxter jerked when Addison shot to his feet, then started to pace along the edge of the stream. "I know we weren't supposed to question, but my DNA is set so I do a bit of independent thinking as an officer. It's not my fault the genetic mutations the scientists brought into being are starting to think for themselves. We aren't robots, Baxter. We're real, living, breathing people, and we don't deserve to be sacrificed for their arrogance and greed."

"I'm not arguing with you about that. All I'm saying is what did Lopez offer you that was so attractive you chose to desert rather than stay?"

"He offered us asylum. He offered us a home where we don't have to fight every minute for people who don't care whether we live or die." Addison swung around to look at him. "Lopez told me if I wanted to be free, he'd give me the keys to unlock my chains."

"And you said yes," Baxter said, not completely surprised that Addison had taken the offer.

Addison propped his fists on his hips. "Fuck yes, I took that offer. I know there'll be a debt I have to pay eventually. I know Lopez doesn't make offers like that without strings, but I can't watch you die, Baxter. If by putting myself in debt to Lopez, I keep you alive, I'm willing to sell my soul to that devil any day of the week."

After pushing himself from the tree, Baxter stumbled over to Addison and threw his arms around his lover. He crushed his lips to Addison's, tasting their tears as they mingled. He demanded entrance, and Addison opened to him. It was awkward because they were in full gear, but Baxter did his best to get them as close as humanly possible amid the rifles, knives and various other weapons they still carried.

When his lungs were burning from lack of oxygen, he broke off their kiss, resting his forehead against Addison's. "I guess I never realized just how my injuries bothered you."

"They fucking wrecked me, Baxter. The man I loved was in a coma, and no one was holding out any hope you'd come out of it. While I cussed out every doctor I saw, the Trues were acting like you were just a little insect whose death didn't matter in the grand scheme of the war. You were just one more mutant that didn't survive. They thought of your death as culling a defective member of our kind."

Baxter kept his mouth shut because that was exactly how the scientists and military people thought of the GEs dying. The strongest of the DNA strains were those who survived several years of fighting. They cultivated those strands to create new generations of GEs. Addison knew that as well, yet he could see how the knowledge had torn a hole in Addison's heart.

"I love you, Addison," he whispered.

172

Chapter Fourteen

Addison shuddered.

Back when he'd sat next to Baxter's bed in the hospital and stared at the silent man lying there, Addison had thought he'd never hear those words, and it was that fear that had driven him to accept Lopez's offer. It was a deal he'd made, knowing whether Baxter woke up or whether he died, Addison would find his way to Mexico within a year or two.

The moment Baxter had gone down, he'd decided it was time to escape their fate because he didn't believe in the war they were fighting. He didn't respect the people they were fighting for. The only people he loved and cared for were the men in his unit, especially the big, quiet soldier who'd been created to be a grunt.

"I love you more than anything else in the world, Baxter," Addison confessed against Baxter's lips. "If that means I have to fight in one of Lopez's wars, then I'll do so, because it means you'll be able to run along the beach and play with the kids in the ocean."

Baxter snorted. "Like I'd let you go anywhere without me. No, when we cross over into Mexico, Lopez gains two GEs to fight his petty battles. I bet the others will feel the same way, but you have to tell them what kind of deal you made, Addison. They need to know the entire story, so they can make their own decisions."

Addison nodded. "I know. I was planning on doing that before we reached the border. My deal with Lopez works no matter how many people come with me. He'll take us all in, and it's just my debt to be paid. You don't owe him anything."

He stumbled slightly when Baxter shoved him away. When he got his balance again, Baxter poked him in the chest.

"What debt you incur is my debt as well. You did all of this because of me, and I'll help you pay for our freedom, Addison. I'm not some kind of helpless creature you're moving to higher ground to keep safe. I'm a soldier, and I've got the scars to prove I can survive whatever life throws at me." Baxter touched the scar that crawled along the right side of his head like a line of drunken ants before tapping his cheek under his eye.

The doctors hadn't been concerned about looks when they'd stitched Baxter up. All they'd been worried about was keeping his brains in his skull at the time. They hadn't wanted to risk losing any useful information they might gain from the organ if Baxter died.

Addison breathed deeply, acknowledging to himself that he'd always known Baxter would react this way when he got around to telling him about Lopez. He didn't want to think about Baxter fighting any more. He truly wanted his lover to play with Little Bit in the sand instead.

"I understand, Baxter, and I promise not to treat you like you're fragile. I haven't done that since your first injury. I'm not going to start now." He pushed up on his tiptoes to give Baxter a quick peck on the cheek.

His lover encircled his waist then pulled him tight to his chest. "Do you think we're far enough away they won't hear us if I fuck you?" Baxter whispered into his ear.

"Shit!" Addison swore softly.

Baxter started to unhook his gear.

Addison knew it wasn't a good idea. They had more to worry about than being caught by their own men. A UEA patrol could show up at any time. He and Baxter should keep their senses uncluttered by lust and need.

Yet he knew he'd always be aware of Baxter, no matter what kind of danger they were in. Also, his lover's other senses were growing stronger to compensate for the loss of sight in his eye. If Baxter was cool with them doing it in the clearing, then Addison would go with the flow.

Baxter brushed a kiss over his lips. "Trust me, Addison. I wouldn't do anything that could get us caught. Besides, it's going to be fast."

"All right."

The last word had barely escaped his mouth before he found himself pressed face first against a tree, his pants around his ankles and Baxter's spit-coated fingers buried in his ass.

Gasping, he braced his hands on the rough bark, then tilted his hips, silently begging for more.

Baxter bit the nape of Addison's neck, accepting Addison's submission almost like an alpha wolf would from his mate. Addison moaned as Baxter shoved three fingers inside. The burn of having his hole stretched and used so roughly caused his own erection to flag slightly.

"Just a second, love," Baxter murmured. "Let me find it."

He hit Addison's gland and electricity raced along every nerve in Addison's body.

"Holy fuck," he breathed, as he chased after Baxter's touch each time his lover eased away.

Baxter chuckled, and his warm breath washed over Addison's skin, drawing another shiver from him. The bite of the bark against the tender skin of his cock seemed to drive Addison even crazier, though after a few minutes of that, he pushed his lower half farther away from the wood. Rubbing himself raw would be hell as they continued their journey.

Baxter made sure to hit his gland with his knuckle with each stroke until Addison was rocking and moaning, lost in the sensations. Finally, Addison reached a point where he wanted more.

"Baxter, please, I need you," he begged.

"I'm always here for you, Addison. You never have to ask."

175

He groaned as Baxter slid his fingers from him. Holding his breath, Addison waited for the moment when he'd be claimed completely by the man he loved.

"Breath and try to relax. Remember, pushing while I shove in will help," Baxter advised before Addison felt him move back in position to cover his back.

Addison tried to follow Baxter's instructions as the pressure grew. It felt three times as big as Baxter's fingers, and he scrambled to hold on to something before he ordered Baxter to stop.

But his lover didn't stop until Addison could feel the coarse piece of Velcro from Baxter's pants scrape against the surface of his ass. They both released their breaths in a tangled sigh of sound when Baxter was seated deep inside Addison.

He wrenched his head around, needing to feel Baxter's mouth on his. Baxter knew exactly what Addison wanted. He sipped from Addison's lips like he was a glass of the rarest wine, and while they kissed, Baxter began to move.

Each thrust in and out seemed to last a lifetime, building the pleasure and need with every moment. He whined when Baxter wrapped his hand around Addison's cock, surrounding him with more sensation.

After folding his arms high on the tree, Addison rested his forehead on them, content to let Baxter control what was happening. Soon his lover's movements became jerky, and Addison's own climax hovered on the edge of his conscious.

"Come for me, Addison," Baxter requested, and because Addison could never deny Baxter anything, he did.

He bowed his back and painted the craggy wood in front of him with strings of his cum. The only coherent thought he had was he hoped none got on his clothes. He didn't have any more clean uniform, having decided that they needed the room in their packs for food, water and ammo.

Baxter slammed into him a few more times before he flooded Addison's channel with hot cum. He loved the way it felt as it filled him, then started to drip from his ass when Baxter slid out.

They stripped, quickly washing up in the chilly stream. After drying, Addison dressed, and kissed Baxter before they headed back to where the others camped.

The children were already asleep by the time they returned. Patterson and Gephardt were on watch while the others were spread out around the clearing. Addison checked with the two on guard before he joined Baxter at their blankets.

* * * *

In the morning, they regrouped and headed out. Baxter drove the truck this time, and Addison rode up front again. It was important that he be available if they ever were stopped.

He didn't mention his plans to the rest of the men until they were only a few hours away from the border. They'd had a few close calls, but no one had pulled them over to check them out.

Once they stopped for the evening, Addison gathered the rest of their little band. The last of their food was passed around so everyone had something to eat.

"All right, I need to talk to everyone. We only have a couple more klicks before we hit the border, and I guess this is the time to tell you all what my plan is to get us into Mexico." Addison sat next to Baxter by the truck tire.

Patterson shrugged. "It's up to you, sir. We're here because we trust you, and if we have to fight our way across, then we'll do so. As long as the kids get out okay, then I'm fine with whatever."

The others nodded, though Dash and Mariah didn't look convinced. He smiled at them.

"I don't think it'll come down to that. When I first decided if we were to live, we had to run, I made a deal with Lopez." He waited for the explosion, but surprisingly there wasn't one.

"Lopez, as in the head of the Mexican West Coast Cartel. As in the most dangerous man next to the supreme commander and the ruler of the UEA?" Synder asked, looking puzzled.

"Yes."

"How the hell did you get a hold of him to be able to make a deal?" Patterson shifted where he sat, finishing up his food.

Addison glanced over at Baxter before saying, "Actually, one of his people approached me. It was shortly after Baxter was injured, and the docs couldn't tell me whether he'd live or die. AFF didn't care about him. It really didn't matter to them what happened to him."

He pushed to his feet and started to pace. "But it mattered to me, and that's when I realized we needed to leave if we were going to survive. The deal I made with Lopez is this— he'll allow us to cross over into his territory and live there. But if he needs me to do something, I have to go and do it. It's like having his own personal GE at his beck and call."

"Two GEs at his beck and call," Baxter stated. "I don't care if we're safe or not. I'm not letting you out of my sight."

"Neither are any of us." Markeo gestured to the entire unit. "We're a package deal, sir. He wants one, he gets us all. Hell, we have a debt to pay him as well for letting us in."

"Will we have to do anything?" Dash glanced over at Mariah.

Addison shook his head. "No. He doesn't know how many are coming, but it doesn't matter. Our deal was for everyone, but only I was going to have to pay the debt."

"And that's changed now." Baxter stood, then walked over to him. "Lopez will get an entire trained GE unit to help with whatever he wants."

Looking around the group, he saw all of them nodding. He should've known they wouldn't let him shoulder the burden of their freedom alone. "Thank you," he said, feeling a little choked up.

Baxter rested his hand on his shoulder. "You've done a lot of things for us, Addison, like keeping the Trues off our backs and doing all of the planning for this to get us somewhere we have a chance of living a full life."

It was the truth, and they all knew it. If they'd stayed with the AFF, they would have been dead within the month—Tilton hated them, and he'd go out of his way to give them the most dangerous assignments almost guaranteed to get them killed.

Addison setting up this opportunity had saved them, and they would pay their lieutenant back by doing pretty much anything for him.

"All right then. We'll get some rest tonight. In the morning, we'll head for the border. I managed to get a message to Lopez to expect us at this crossing at noon. Hopefully, he'll be there."

The kids went to their beds, and the men set up watch times. Addison sat back on the ground next to the tire, legs crossed and hands resting limply in his lap. He needed time to think through what was going to happen tomorrow. There was a chance Lopez would renege on his deal, but Addison didn't think that he would. There were a lot of bad things said about Lopez and his vicious, ironclad control of the west coast of Mexico, but the one thing everyone said was that when Lopez gave his word, he kept it.

Addison was holding that truth close to his heart. He didn't know what they would do if they had to fight their way through the armies at the border. Well, he knew what they'd do—they'd fight until they couldn't anymore, then make sure the children were safe.

GEs weren't afraid of dying, even if they were running from it right now. His men were indifferent to death, as long as it was for some cause worthy of their sacrifice. He didn't look at Baxter when his lover dropped next to him.

"We should get some sleep, Addison. We have the last shift before we bug out in the morning." Baxter started arranging their sleeping bags.

"Yeah." He took a deep breath, letting go of his tension and giving up tomorrow to the universe, knowing there was no way he could control the future. The scientists hadn't figured out how to program mutated GEs to do that yet.

Addison curled his body around Baxter then brushed a kiss over the nape of Baxter's neck. "I love you, Baxter."

"Love you, too, sir," Baxter mumbled.

Addison smiled, content in his soul as he drifted asleep.

* * * *

The next day, as they were approaching the border, Addison wiped his sweaty palms on his pants. This was where things could go to hell very quickly if Lopez hadn't upheld his end of the bargain. Addison drove up to the guardhouse, and he watched as the uniformed man came out to walk over.

The rest of the men and the kids were in the back of the truck, ready to fight if it came to that. Addison silently prayed that it wouldn't.

"Name," the man demanded.

"Lieutenant Addison."

Baxter stayed silent, following Addison's orders.

The guard eyed him with undisguised interest, but didn't react other than that. "All right, Lieutenant, I have a packet for you, then you're free to cross."

Baxter heaved a relieved sigh, but Addison didn't relax. Things could still go wrong. They weren't completely safe until they were deep into Lopez territory.

The soldier reappeared carrying a large manila envelope, which he handed to Addison. "Everything you need is in there, along with a phone. Our mutual friend says you must call him once you are thirty klicks from the border. He would like to welcome you personally. There is a map to a town on the coast that you might be interested in checking out."

"Thank you," Addison replied.

The man's bright smile caught him a little off guard, but he returned it with one of his own.

"It is our thanks that we must be giving to you, Lieutenant. Just your presence will bring safety to many who can't protect themselves." After stepping away from the truck, he gestured to the man operating the gate to open it.

Addison drove through the checkpoint while Baxter emptied the envelope.

"What's in there?" He continued down the road, planning to stop exactly where Lopez wanted him.

"There are official documents for all of us, even the kids." Baxter shuffled through the piles. "Here's the phone."

Addison took it, then set it on the dashboard.

"This is the map he must've been talking about," Baxter muttered, unfolding it. "Wow. Looks like this village is right on the ocean. I bet the kids will enjoy playing in the sand."

He didn't doubt that they would. "As long as the village is safe for them, I'm pretty sure we could stay there. At least that's how it sounded."

"Right."

Things looked like they were working out. They would meet their benefactor before heading for their new home. Addison reached out to take Baxter's hand in his.

"Are you ready to start a new life with me?"

"Yes, sir. Let's go greet it with open hearts and minds. It's a new adventure and a better future than we had back home."

Addison couldn't have agreed more.

Epilogue

Addison walked down to the beach where the men and kids were playing. It wasn't just the ones they had brought with them—the village kids had joined in after they'd gotten over their fear of the strange soldiers. He smiled as he thought of the six months they'd been living in *Aldea de la arena blanco*, or *Arena Blanco*, which is what the inhabitants of the village called it.

He stepped out onto the white sand, which gave the village its name, and strolled over to where a large group milled about. Glancing around, he saw Baxter crouched next to Little Bit as they stared intently into a tidal pool. Addison wondered what they were studying so closely.

Markeo and Dash sat a little ways down the beach, chatting about something. Their relationship was moving along slowly because neither man seemed to want to rush it. Addison thought it was a good idea. The best relationships were ones built on layers of trust, and those layers took time to create.

Baxter looked up at him and smiled. Addison winked, then gestured for him to join the group. Baxter swept Little Bit into his arms before strolling over to Addison.

"Markeo, Dash, could you join us, please?" Addison called to the couple.

After everyone was gathered around, Addison said, "I just got off the phone with Señor Lopez."

A sad look came into the children's eyes because they knew when Lopez called, their big guardian angels usually had to leave for a while.

"He has a job for us down around the border between

north and south Mexico. The good news is it should only take a week at the most to clean up the problem."

"The bad news?" Dash asked from where he stood close to Markeo.

"It's going to take all but one of us to do it." Addison pulled a piece of paper from his back pocket. "I checked the schedule and it looks like it's Markeo's turn to stay behind. The rest of you need to be ready to move by oh-eight-hundred tomorrow morning."

He could see the relief in Dash's eyes and understood how the young man felt. It was the same happiness he got whenever it was Baxter's turn to stay behind. As much as he loved his soldier—and knew he could take care of himself—Addison hated having Baxter anywhere he ran the risk of getting hurt because it was no longer just Baxter's life on the line—it was Addison's heart as well.

"Will do, sir."

They scattered back to what they were doing, and he went back to the tidal pool with Baxter. They rarely had to fight anymore, and Addison took comfort in the knowledge that all his men would live normal lives. They would have families, and die of old age in their *haciendas* instead of in the middle of a battlefield as they'd been bred to do.

Addison thought about their journey and how it had all worked out. His unit was thriving alongside the villagers, and he got to go to sleep every night with the man he loved by his side. There was nothing quite as freeing as that knowledge.

Home Sweet Home

Excerpt

Chapter One

Thirteen years later

"You have everything?"

After tossing his last bag into the back of his truck, Yancey turned to look at his brother. "Yes. The rest of my stuff you can ship out after I get settled."

Brody didn't look convinced. "Are you sure this is the right thing to do? You could open your own practice around here."

"I know, but Juan isn't here, and it's time we start being together. I still love him." Yancey shrugged. "I'm not sure if you and Tony hoped it was puppy love between us, or if you just wanted us both to see the world before we settled down with each other."

"Would it be wrong to say a little of both?" Brody smiled. "I think I was the one who hoped it was just puppy love, and for no other reason than that I didn't believe people could fall in love so early in life."

"I was the one who wanted you and Juan to taste the world outside our ranch before you chose each other. I could see how solid the two of you were with each other, but you needed to learn about the way things work out in the real world." Tony used air quotes when he said real.

Yancey laughed. "You probably didn't think it would lead to Juan living all the way across the country, doing something kind of foreign to you."

Tony slid his arm around Brody's waist, then leaned into his side. "If he were an investment banker, then that would be foreign to me. He rides horses, just in a fancier saddle than I do. So we're closer than you'd think."

"Does Juan know you're coming?" Brody still didn't look convinced that it was the best move on Yancey's part.

Yancey shook his head. "No. He only knows that I'm coming out for a visit. He doesn't have any clue that I'll be living a mile down the road from the stables he works at. I didn't want him to know until I could tell him face-to-face. I'm hoping he'll be pleasantly surprised."

"Knowing Juan, he'll go crazy about it. There's no doubt in my mind that Juan loves you just as much now as he did when he was sixteen."

Yancey wasn't so sure about that. There had been times when Juan had missed important events because he'd had to ride in different shows. Yancey tried to be supportive—Juan was building a career, and needed to put on a good showing in order to get clients. Yet lately, Yancey felt like Juan was putting his career before their relationship, and he didn't want that to happen.

That was why he'd chosen to buy out a retiring veterinarian whose practice was only a mile away from the barn Juan rode and worked at in Virginia. He wanted to be close to the man he loved so they could get reacquainted. He needed to learn who this new Juan was, and see if their love would be strong enough to survive the changes in both of them.

"You better head out. Don't want to throw you off schedule. Take your time though. There's no need to rush, right?" Brody hugged him tight.

"No. I'm leaving here early, and I told Dr Behan I would at his place in two weeks, so I have plenty of time. Might make a stop or two along the way." Yancey absorbed the strength in Brody's embrace.

All his life he'd looked up to his older brother, and relied on him to help make everything right in his world. Now it was time for Yancey to branch out on his own.

"You'll make sure to call us when you stop for the night, right?" Brody checked.

"I will call you every day, Brody, but you know what? You have to let me go at some point." Yancey smiled. "You do realise that from the time I was fifteen until I turned eighteen, I was pretty much on my own, and I took care of myself. I haven't lost that ability. Though this time I won't have to sell myself if I run out of money."

Brody grimaced at the reminder of what Yancey had been doing when they'd found each other again. Yancey knew his brother hated the idea of him being a rent boy, but it had been the only way Yancey had been able to make enough money to survive on the streets of Austin.

While Yancey wasn't particularly proud of what he'd done, he wasn't embarrassed by it. It was what it was, and he couldn't change the past. He'd learnt his lesson about running away.

Tony wrapped his arm around Brody's waist, giving Yancey a bright smile. "Don't worry, I have ways of keeping him distracted."

Yancey rolled his eyes. "I don't want to know any of those ways, Tony. I'm perfectly happy being ignorant of your sex life."

"You might get some good tips for when you and Juan get together," Tony joked, wiggling his eyebrows.

"For God's sake, can we not talk about this?" Brody

looked put out by the whole conversation.

"I'm just saying that Brody won't be calling you every hour to find out how you're doing on your trip." Tony tightened his grip on Brody. "He's dealing with 'empty nest' syndrome, and you haven't even left the driveway."

Yancey opened his truck door, then slid behind the wheel and shut the door. He was excited to be setting off on his trip—he'd been looking forward to heading out east after he'd settled the deal with Dr Behan.

But really, it was finally getting to spend as much time with Juan as he wanted that got him thrilled to be starting out on the long drive.

"Hey, don't forget to stop and say goodbye to Les and Randy," Tony reminded him.

"I won't. It's not like you all won't be out to see Juan and me in a couple weeks. The Hampton Classic starts then, and I know Les is planning on visiting. He's looking for some more horses for Juan and Edward."

Brody nodded. "I think Les is determined to start another stables, but not out here."

"Do you think he'll want to move back?" Yancey couldn't see either Les or Randy living anywhere except Wyoming.

More books from
T.A. Chase

A moment in time can be the most pivotal one in our lives.

Home is sweetest when it's the one person you can't live without.

T.A. CHASE

An angel must decide if losing his heart is worth it

THE FOUR HORSEMEN

PEACE

When falling in love means risking everything, an angel must decide if losing his heart is worth it.

SAY THE WORD 'LOVE' OUT LOUD BEFORE IT'S TOO LATE FOR ANYTHING OTHER THAN GOODBYE.

DELAROSA SECRETS

COLD TRUTH

T. A. CHASE

When the truth comes out, Victor and Bieito must decide how strong their love really is.

About the Author

T.A. Chase

There is beauty in every kind of love, so why not live a life without boundaries? Experiencing everything the world offers fascinates TA and writing about the things that make each of us unique is how she shares those insights. When not writing, TA's watching movies, reading and living life to the fullest.

T.A. Chase loves to hear from readers. You can find contact information, website details and an author profile page at https://www.pride-publishing.com/

PUBLISHING